Skipton Parish Church
1951-52.

PRESENTED
∴ TO ∴

John Mills

for regular

attendance at

Bible Class

R. L. ALLAN & SON. LTD., 141 SAUCHIEHALL ST., GLASGOW.

WINGS OF ADVENTURE

by

T. C. BRIDGES

THE CHILDREN'S PRESS
LONDON AND GLASGOW

PRINTED IN GREAT BRITAIN

CHAPTER ONE

A BUSMAN'S HOLIDAY

AIR CADET WILLIAM HAWKINS lay back in a long cane chair and stared gloomily out of the window.

With his slim figure, very fair hair and clear blue eyes he seemed a mere child. It was when you looked a second time and noted the firm lips, the tiny lines about the eyes and the lean, wiry strength of him you realised there was more of the hardened man about him than his seventeen years should have shown.

On the face of it there was nothing to account for his gloom, for he looked as fit as any young fellow could be; while as for the weather, it was as perfect as only an English summer day can be.

The door burst open and a big young man strode in. "Hallo, Billy!" he exclaimed genially, and stopped short. "Why, what's the matter? You look as if you had lost a half-crown and found sixpence."

"And that's the way I feel, Len," Billy answered. "I'm fed up."

Len Holton stood quite still and stared at the other. "Fed up!" he repeated in a scandalised tone. "Not with flying, Billy?"

"No, you ass. With the Flying Service."

Len Holton shook his head.

"What's the difference?" he demanded.

7

" You'd know if you were in it," replied Bill savagely. " All drill and discipline and dressing up. A few hours in the machine-shop as a treat and a trip once in a blue moon. For two pins I'd chuck the whole shooting match."

Len dropped his big body into a chair opposite Billy and was silent for a little. Then he nodded.

" I see your point of view, Billy, and no doubt it comes specially hard on you because you were flying at an age when most kids are learning a bicycle. But we all have to go through the mill, and if you can stick it out you'll do well in the long run."

" That's the trouble. I can't stick it, Len. And I don't quite see why I should. I haven't a relation except my brother Bob, and he's safe at school. I've a mind to chuck it and see if I can't get in with one of the big commercial flying firms. After all, I can fly."

" You can, Billy," allowed Len. " For your age there isn't a better pilot in the country. But take my tip and don't chuck a certainty until you can see another."

Holton's earnestness had its effect.

" All right, Len," Billy answered. " I'll try to stick it out for a bit longer. But if I do get the chance of a real job I'm going to jump at it."

" I've got one for you to-day," said Len.

" A job!"

" Don't get excited. It's only a bit of a fly. How much more leave have you got?"

" Three days."

" Plenty of time. A chap rang up just now

8

to ask us if we could flip him down to Tarnmouth. Seems he wants to catch the liner which sails for Rio to-night. I'm booked to take the mail plane to Dublin, Jerry Goode is in bed with a chill, and we haven't any one to do the job."

" What about Merton?" cut in Billy.

" Merton is here, but the boss won't trust him with one of the new Dolphins."

Billy sprang up.

" One of the Dolphins! Len, if there's a job I've longed for it is to pilot one of those new planes. And to be trusted with one of them is the biggest compliment you could pay me."

Len smiled at his eagerness.

" Right you are then, Billy. And since there isn't too much time to spare you might as well come across to the hangar at once and go over the machine with me."

Billy was keen as mustard. The Dolphin, an amphibian, was the latest production from the works of Messrs. Webster & Walton, and Len Holton himself had had more than a bit to do with the designing. It was not a big machine, but a new-type engine of 750 horse-power gave it a speed of nearly 300 miles an hour. It climbed in marvellous fashion, and was extremely handy and economical. Being an amphibian it could, of course, alight on water or on land at will.

For Billy the next hour slipped by like five minutes, and he was surprised when Len glanced at his watch and told him that it was time to get away. Billy went with him to another hangar where the big mail plane was housed, and saw the mechanics wheel it out. Len climbed in.

" So long, Billy," he said. " See you to-morrow."

He taxied off, rose, wheeled and raised his hand, and Billy watched him climb the hills on the far side of the aerodrome and drive upwards into the blue. Billy turned to see two men coming across the brown turf towards him. One was Peter Fulton, the business manager of the aerodrome, the other was short, dark, foreign-looking. He had a broad, white scar all across his left cheek which, together with his coffee complexion and his very dark eyes, gave him a some-what sinister appearance.

" Hawkins," said Fulton, " here is your passenger. Let me introduce you. Mr. William Hawkins—Señor Juan Pecos."

Pecos stared at Billy then turned to Fulton.

" It is not that you send me up with this child?" he said sharply. The faintest shade of pink showed under Billy's tan; as for Fulton, he hastened to make peace.

" Mr. Hawkins is not so young as he looks, señor. He's a cadet in His Majesty's Air Force. You may take it from me that a more competent pilot could not be found."

Pecos still stared at Billy. Then suddenly he thrust out his hand.

" I am sorry," he said. " I see you not young as I think. You will do."

" What time is your boat?" asked Billy. " What time does she start, I mean.

" The boat—yes, the ship. She start at eight."
Billy glanced at his watch.

" It's six now. We had better be getting on,"
he said and walked towards the hangar. He did
not like the looks of his passenger and the man's
manners were worse than his looks. But Billy
was not worrying about that. His thoughts were
centred entirely upon the delights of flying this
new machine over a distance of something like
two hundred miles.

The Dolphin was all ready and waiting; her
tank was filled, and every stay, nut and bolt had
been gone over by the mechanics in attendance.

" She's a topper," said Billy to Fulton.
" Jolly good of you to let me take her."

" The boot's on the other foot!" laughed
Fulton. " I needn't ask you to be good to her.
And "—he whispered in Billy's ear—" you'll
see she's properly locked up for the night. There
are gadgets about her we don't want every one
to examine."

" Trust me," said Billy. " Are you sending
a mechanic with me?"

" No. Fact is this passenger of yours has no
end of baggage; and you don't want any more
weight."

Billy nodded. " It doesn't matter. Is the
stuff well stowed?"

" You needn't worry about that," was the
reply. " It's all fast." He turned to Pecos.
" Get aboard, sir," he said. Pecos climbed into
his seat behind Billy, Fulton swung the propeller,
and the great engine broke into roaring life. In

less than half a minute the Dolphin was in the air.

" My hat, she can shift!" said Billy to himself.

The Dolphin's power, the way she climbed, her steadiness, and, above all, her comparative silence filled him with delighted amazement. He was so pleased and interested that for the time he quite forgot his passenger and gave himself up to the joy of handling this wonderful plane.

He climbed until he reached the three-thousand-foot level, where he found a favouring wind; then he turned south-west and let her rip. The pointer on the gauge rose till it indicated 200 miles, and that without giving her anything like full gas.

Suddenly he became aware that his passenger wished to speak to him and slipped the telephone head-piece over his ears. " I have changed my mind," Pecos said in his queer, clipped English. " I do not want to go to Tarnmouth." Billy stared. He could hardly believe his ears. " Do you mean that you want to go back to Marchester?" he demanded.

" No, it is not that I wish to return. I wish you to take me to an island which is called Wreak Island. You know it?"

" I know it all right," said Billy, " but I can't take you there. You must understand that I have my orders from Mr. Calvert and they are to take you to Tarnmouth."

" But I am the passenger, the one who pays. You will take the orders from me, Meester Hawkins."

"That is out of the question," returned Billy curtly. "My job is to take you to Tarnmouth and that is what I intend to do."

Billy felt a sudden sharp prod in the side, and realised that Pecos had pulled an automatic and rammed the muzzle against his ribs.

"Do my order or I shoot," snarled the man. Billy's first impression was that the man had gone mad, but a second glance showed him that he was in a mighty tight place. The man meant to steal the Dolphin and the thought made him boil. For an instant he wondered whether it would be possible to leave the controls, swing round and stun Pecos with a punch in the jaw, but it did not take him more than three seconds to see that this was out of the question. His only chance was to pretend to obey the fellow's orders and trust to luck to get back on him. "If you shoot me you have a long way to fall," he said quietly. "Put that gun away and tell me plainly what you want." Pecos removed his pistol muzzle from Billy's ribs but still held the weapon pointed at him. "I have told you that which I require," he growled. "It is to fly to Wreak Island. You obey what I say?" Billy shrugged. "It seems I haven't any choice," he said, "but there's just one objection to your plan. There is no landing-place on the island."

"You will land upon the sea," answered Pecos. "The airplane has the floats to swim on."

"You seem to know all about it," said Billy quietly, "but there's one thing I want to

13

ask: What happens to me when you get to Wreak? If you are going to shoot me when you get there, you may just as well do the job now. Then I shall have the satisfaction of taking you with me." Pecos' little eyes had an evil gleam, but he swallowed his rage. " You will be safe," he promised. " I give you my word of a gentleman."

" I don't think!" muttered Billy, but in a tone which Pecos could not hear. " All right," he said aloud. " I suppose I must make the best of it. Let me see. Wreak Island lies to the west. I'll have a glance at the map so as to get my compass course. Please hand me the map out of that locker to your right."

The ruse worked. Pecos laid the pistol on the seat beside him and leaned over to open the locker. The moment his head was turned Billy pulled over the joystick and Pecos screamed as the whole machine tilted and dropped like a falling meteor. The scream was cut off as if by the turning of a tap, and Billy felt a thud as the man's body struck the back of his own seat.

For nearly a thousand feet the plane fell like a stone before Billy got control again and flattened her out. Then, and not till then, did he glance round. Blood was flowing from a cut on Pecos' head, but the man was more scared than hurt, and Billy saw that he was reviving. He glanced to the right, saw the automatic on the floor, and, snatching it up, thrust it into his own pocket.

" Pulled his teeth, anyhow," he said. " And

now, you dirty dog, you're for the high jump and don't you forget it." He pulled the control over and the plane rose steeply, so that Pecos, who was trying to get to his feet, fell over backwards.

" I kill you," he screamed as he struggled to regain his balance.

" Try it, my beauty!" grinned Billy.

What that plane did in the next five minutes no one but an airman could describe. It stood on its head and its tail, it rolled like a motor-boat in a gale, it bucked like a bad-tempered bronco. It rose like a rocket and fell like a leaf.

Before he had finished, Pecos' face was the colour of lead, his eyes were almost popping out of his head, and he was very sick. His lips moved, and though Billy could not hear what he said, he could make a pretty good guess. " Yes, you can pray all you like," he said, " but I'm not taking any more chances with a scorpion like you. You're going to be tied up good and tight before you're fit to sting again."

He glanced down. The plane was flying over a great expanse of lonely moorland, and a couple of miles ahead Billy saw a long, level ridge with a flat top which looked as if it would make a landing-place.

" No rocks, I hope," he said to himself. " And I don't think there's much heather. Looks all right to me."

He descended and, picking his place, dropped lightly on to the ridge. The wheels touched ground, the plane shot forward, then suddenly there was a crunch and she stopped with a heavy jerk.

" Now I've done it," growled Billy. " Just the rock I didn't see."

But the first thing was to put Pecos beyond reach of further mischief. Out came a length of cord and Billy set to work to tie up his passenger. The man's eyes were evil as those of a striking snake, but luckily for Billy he was in no shape to put up a fight. Billy tied his thumbs behind his back, lashed his ankles together, then set to finding out what had happened to the plane.

It was as he had thought. The off-wheel had struck a piece of granite hidden by a clump of heather and was badly buckled. Billy saw at once that he could not rise again until he had fitted a new wheel. " Putrid luck!" he grumbled. " And, of course, I'm miles from help."

It certainly looked like it, for all around him lay great stretches of moorland. It was a very beautiful view, but at the moment Billy would have preferred the ugliest clump of smoke stacks. The more he thought of the situation the less he liked it.

Billy's blue eyes were clouded as he turned slowly round and carefully examined every bit of the surrounding country. Away off to the west was a valley, the bottom of which was heavily wooded and from among the trees arose a faint curl of blue smoke.

" A house, anyhow," remarked Billy. He glanced back at Pecos. " I suppose I'll have to take the blighter with me," he growled. " If I leave him here and someone comes along, goodness knows what tale he'll pitch. And if he once gets loose he'll probably smash up the whole bag of tricks.''

He went back to the plane and cut the lashings from Pecos' ankles. '' You're coming with me,'' he said. '' Stir your stumps!''

The glare in the dago's eyes was like that in a mad dog's, but the man had had a taste of Billy's quality. He obeyed orders, and they started.

CHAPTER TWO

THE MIND READER

WALKING across a pathless moor is never the easiest job in the world. The wiry heather catches your feet and you stumble over loose stones.

Billy had sensible shoes, but Pecos was wearing the pointed, thin-soled abominations which his sort thinks to be smart, and he made very heavy weather of it.

Billy had not dared untie his hands, so when Pecos stumbled he could not save himself, and unless Billy caught him in time he generally went flat on his face.

Half a mile of this sort of thing drove Billy nearly frantic. '' See here,'' he said, '' I'm not going to spend the rest of the day picking you out of bog holes. I'm going to leave you under these rocks until I get back.''

Pecos stared at him sullenly but made no objection, and Billy tied him up again and left him under a granite ledge which would give some sort of shelter and would, he hoped, hide him from the eyes of any wandering moorman.

After that it was better going, but the distance was greater than Billy had thought, and the sun was down before he reached the last ridge above the valley and saw the house lying beneath him.

He pulled up short and gazed at it in some astonishment. "Rum-looking place," he remarked to himself. "More like a prison than a dwelling-house."

He was right. The house, built of grey granite, was massive, and the enclosure in which it stood was surrounded by a ten-foot stone wall in which was only one gate, a solid-looking affair of heavy timber. Behind the house was a vegetable garden, but in front nothing but grass. Not a flower or a shrub was to be seen in the whole place.

"I wonder what sort of crack built that," said Billy thoughtfully.

He hurried down the hillside and a few minutes later found himself at the gate. A heavy bell-chain hung beside it. Billy pulled and at once a tremendous baying broke out from the other side. Then the door quivered as something sprang at it.

"That's a number-one-sized dog," observed Billy as he felt for Pecos' automatic. "It doesn't sound a bit pretty or nice."

"Get back, Bouncer!" came a gruff voice, and Billy heard a key turn in the lock. The door opened about a foot and a huge man with the surliest-looking face that Billy had ever seen appeared in the opening. Behind him was a mastiff about the size of a small donkey. " What d'ye want?" growled the man in a voice that rolled like distant thunder.

" Help," replied Billy briefly. " I'm an airman. I came down on the moor, damaged the plane, and can't get up again without help."

The giant gateman stared at him in silence. " I don't believe you," he said at last. " You're one of the gang."

Billy lost patience. " Is this a lunatic asylum?" he asked sarcastically.

" Give me any more of your brass and I'll turn the dog on ye," threatened the man. " I'm paid to keep the gang out o' here, and I does it."

Billy was boiling, but he bit off an angry retort. " See here," he said, " I haven't the faintest notion what you mean by the gang. I'm a Britisher, and a cadet in the Air Force. I call on you in His Majesty's name to give me help, and you will refuse me at your peril."

Billy's tone impressed the fellow; he scratched his great head. " I'll ask the master," he said. " You wait outside till I brings him."

" No need to bring me, Croker," came a strong, clear voice, and there stepped past Croker the most remarkable man Billy had ever set his eyes on. Six feet high, he was as slim and vigorous-looking as a man of thirty, yet his thick hair was quite white. He had a beaked nose and a pair of blazing blue eyes, wonderful eyes which seemed to look right through you.

" Who are you, and what do you want?"

While Billy told his story he was conscious that those amazing eyes were fixed upon him in an unwinking stare.

When he had finished the other nodded. " It's all right, Croker," he said calmly. " He is telling the exact truth, though not all of it. Go with him and fetch his prisoner. The plane will be safe where it is till morning. There will be no wind."

" Prisoner," repeated Billy in blank amazement. " I did not say a word about a prisoner! Do you mean you were watching me?"

" I was not watching," said the other simply. " I was busy in my laboratory. My name is Cottle—Mark Cottle. Does that mean anything to you?"

Billy drew a deep breath. " Professor Mark Cottle!" he exclaimed. " The greatest chemist in England! The man who made gold out of mercury! I should rather think it does. All the same," he added, " I don't see how you knew about my prisoner." A whimsical smile crossed the other's face.

" The explanation can wait, the prisoner cannot. Juan Pecos is one of the most dangerous ruffians unhung, and the lives of thousands depend upon getting him safe under lock and key."

Croker stepped forward. " Which way, sir?" he asked of Billy, and now his tone had changed completely and was quite respectful. Professor

Cottle raised his hand. " No, Croker," he said. " I have changed my mind. You stay here, and I will go with Mr. Hawkins."

" Very good, sir," replied Croker, saluting, and Cottle marched out of the gate. " We go west, I think, Mr. Hawkins," he said. Billy was too surprised to do more than nod, and Cottle strode across the rough ground at such a pace that Billy, none too fresh after his recent experiences, had all he could do to keep up with the long strides.

Cottle puzzled him utterly, and for his very life he could not understand how the Professor had come to know about Pecos. There was something almost uncanny about the man, and yet his splendid strength, let alone his great reputation, gave Billy absolute confidence in him. They crossed the ridge and Billy pointed out the rocks under which he had left Pecos. " I only hope we find him," said Cottle in his high, clear voice.

" We'll find him all right," said Billy. " He won't wriggle out of my lashings."

" Not without help," agreed Cottle.

" He's not likely to have been seen, sir," said Billy. " And I gagged him so that he couldn't yell for help."

The Professor stopped short, took from the deep pocket of his shooting coat a pair of small but powerful glasses and focused them on the rock. " And yet I fear he has gone," he said in a lower tone.

" Oh, he can't," cried Billy, and, tired as he was, started to run.

Cottle stopped him. " Go slow, my friend. There is more in this than you yet know of."

Something ominous in his manner gave Billy a chilly feeling. Already he felt himself tangled in a veil of mystery.

" You have a pistol?" said the Professor.

Billy pulled out the automatic he had taken from Pecos, and the other nodded. " Keep it handy," he said, and went forward again.

At last they gained the rock pile, only to find that Cottle was right. There was a patch of grass flattened by Pecos' weight; there were some cut pieces of rope, but of Pecos himself no sign whatever. Cottle stopped and examined the ground. " Two of them," Billy heard him mutter. " I wish I knew which two."

It was some comfort to Billy to know that his companion did not know everything, but just then a new idea flashed across his mind.

" The plane, sir. If Pecos is loose he'll go for her at once. She is a new type and he was mad to get hold of her. Besides, his luggage is in her."

" You are right," said the other curtly. " We had better go and look after her."

" Jove! He takes things coolly," was Billy's inward comment. He was to learn that his new friend was always coolest when things ran most crooked.

From where they stood they could not quite see the plane, for she was hidden by a fold of the hill. Cottle strode on until they reached a point from which she was visible. " All right, so far," he said briefly. " They have not reached her yet. Most likely they are lying doggo. They must have seen us." He stood silent, frowning a little, then turned to Billy. " You can't fly her as she is," he said suddenly.

" No, one wheel is buckled."

" I have spares," said Cottle. " You'd better go back and tell Croker what you need. I'll watch her."

" All right," Billy answered quietly, but as he turned Cottle spoke again. " You're a bit done! Tell Croker to give you the pony to come back," he said. " And see here, don't come straight. Ride round that way "—pointing— " and come up the other side of the hill."

" Very good, sir," replied Billy, and went off. Looking back, he saw Cottle walking towards the plane. " He's a cool card," he said to himself as he hurried on.

Croker was waiting for him at the gate, and was as helpful as he had before been surly. He took Billy straight into a workshop fitted in a style which made the young man gasp. Every sort of spare for car or plane seemed to be at hand, and within a very few minutes Billy had found just what he wanted.

When he came out the pony was ready saddled, and within half an hour from the time of leaving Cottle he was riding rapidly back to rejoin him. Carefully following the directions given him, he made a long round and reached the other side of the hill. He was just beginning to ride up it when a shot rang out followed almost at once by two more.

" So he was right," he muttered as he dug in his heels. " I thought they'd be after the plane."

There was another burst of firing as he cantered up the hill, and following the last shot he heard a shriek. Then he saw the plane and Cottle was lying under it, a pistol in his hand.

Billy jumped off the pony and turned it loose. " You all right, sir?" he called as he ran up.

" All right," answered Cottle calmly. " They have made a hole or two in your canvas but that's about the extent of the damage."

" Then it was one of them who yelled."

" I don't blame him," said Cottle dryly. " I got him in the hand."

" But where are they?" asked Billy.

" In that gorse below. I think that last shot sickened them, and if I'm not much mistaken they are clearing out."

" Can't we collar them?" asked Billy eagerly.

" Not good enough," was the answer. " We should have to advance over open ground, and they'd get us for a certainty. One of them can really shoot."

" Is Pecos with them?"

" No, he's no guts for this sort of thing. Chances are he's lying low, down in the valley. Ah—I told you so!" he added, as two squat, black-haired men suddenly appeared on the lower side of the gorse and went hurrying away downhill. One had his arm in a rough sling.

Billy measured the distance with his eyes, then shook his head. " Out of range, I'm afraid. It's a pity we haven't a rifle."

" A great pity," agreed Cottle. " But since we haven't it can't be helped. Have you the spare for the plane? We mustn't waste time for fog is coming up."

He was right. Already the distances were misted with a fine grey film, so Billy, seeing that there was no time to lose, set to work at once.

Cottle helped him, and in a very short time the plane was herself again. " You have plenty of room to rise," said Cottle. " And I think you can land in my garden. If you flatten out a few cabbages it can't be helped."

As he had said there was plenty of room to rise, and it was only a minute or two before the Dolphin was roaring up above the moor.

Cottle touched Billy's arm and pointed, and down in the valley below Billy saw three men making their way down a narrow path which lay beside a stream. " There are our dear friends," said Cottle in Billy's ear. " They've a car somewhere on the road." He stared at them a moment. " I wish we had a bomb or two," he said harshly.

Billy stared. " You mean you'd use them?"

" With all the pleasure in life," was the answer. " I would kill them with the same amount of compunction as you would put your heel on an adder's head."

" I could put you pretty close over them," said Billy.

" No," said Cottle. " A pistol is useless in a case like this, and you must not risk the plane. Get her down as quickly as you can. Then I think I can do something."

CHAPTER THREE

THE CHASE

IT was not an easy job, even for Billy, to get the Dolphin safely down into the Professor's compound, but he managed it without damage to anything except Croker's cabbages and potatoes. The whole place, Billy now saw, was surrounded with a formidable wall of granite topped with a spiked iron railing. It looked to be safe against anything short of artillery. Cottle saw Billy looking at the wall.

" It doesn't pay me to take any chances," he said significantly. He blew a whistle, and a man came running out. " Make the plane safe, Holmes," ordered the Professor. " And take these cases and put them in the store-room. Tell Gurney I want the car at once."

His orders were obeyed with admirable promptness, and in a very few minutes Billy found himself seated beside Cottle in a two-seater which seemed to have an engine of remarkable power.

Billy himself, like most airmen, was no slouch at driving a car, but here he had to confess that Cottle was his master. They shot away down the rough track at startling speed, and almost before he knew it were on a road. Cottle swung to the right and pressed the accelerator and the car roared up a long, steep slope.

Up and up they went, for here the road climbed right over a high shoulder of the moor, and as they went the air grew thicker and objects began to lose their outline. "Rotten luck," growled Cottle as he slightly slackened speed. "If it wasn't for this infernal fog we should have them on toast. All the same, I'm pretty sure they're making for Lonesand."

"Lonesand. That's opposite Wreak Island, isn't it?"

"Yes. You know it?"

"Wreak's the place where Pecos tried to make me take him."

"Then it's Lonesand for a certainty," said Cottle, sending the car on at increased speed. Next instant came a scrunch of broken glass, two pistol-like reports, the car swerved violently and only Cottle's wonderful quickness saved her from smashing into the bank to the left of the road.

"That's torn it," said Billy as he leapt out. "Yes, both front tyres. I suppose we owe this delicate attention to our friends ahead?"

"Not a doubt of it," replied Cottle. "I ought to have expected it. They've dished us, I'm afraid, for I've only one spare wheel."

Billy was already busy at the back of the car. "Here's a spare tube," he said. "I'll soon have it in."

Cottle caught him by the arm. "That, I fancy, is exactly what the good Pecos expects you to do," he said in a low voice.

"You mean he's laying for us?" whispered Billy.

"That is what is in my mind," replied Cottle with a quick glance round into the thickening fog. "But I think we might diddle them."

As he spoke he had lifted a cushion out of the car and stuck it up endways over the wheel. Round it he flung an overcoat and on top of this his own hat. In the fast thickening fog the resemblance to a man stooping over the tyre was quite good enough to deceive.

"Now to hunt the hunters," murmured Cottle as he drew Billy back under the lee of the right-hand bank.

The road here ran across the open moor, but a little below its level. A bank covered with heather rose three or four feet on each side. Cottle flattened himself in the heather, and Billy did the same. For some minutes nothing happened and Billy was beginning to think that Cottle was for once mistaken when his straining ears caught a rustle somewhere behind the bank against which he lay. Next moment pistols spat crimson flashes through the twilight and bullets thudded on the body of the car. One struck the propped-up cushion and sent it flat in the road.

Billy had his automatic levelled and ready, but Cottle laid a hand on his arm. "Wait!" he whispered in his ear.

Billy heard a voice from the other side of the bank, but the man spoke in Spanish. Billy, who knew a little of the language, heard the words: "I have got one of them."

"But where is the other?" came a second voice.

Again a short pause, then all of a sudden a figure loomed up right above them, and Billy distinctly saw that he had a pistol in his hand.

"The other is here," said Cottle coolly in Spanish, and he and the man fired almost at the same instant. But Cottle must have been just a fraction of a second the quicker of the two, for Billy had only time to jump aside as the fellow came crashing down on the very spot where a moment before he had been lying.

Cottle leaped up the bank, and Billy followed. In the grey gloom they caught a glimpse of two figures running like hares, and Cottle fired so rapidly that the reports ran into one another like those of a machine-gun. But anything like accurate shooting was out of the question and the pair vanished in the foggy twilight.

"Up the road—quickly!" cried Cottle, and he and Billy raced forward. Came the buzz and whirr of a self-starter, then an engine leaped into life. "Shoot!" cried Cottle, and Billy blazed away. He distinctly heard one bullet clang upon metal, but could not even see his target. Rubber-shod wheels tore the road, and the enemy car shot away downhill at tremendous speed.

Cottle shrugged his big shoulders. "They've downed us," he said. "No, it's no use chasing them, Hawkins. It will take us half an hour to make repairs, and by that time it will be dark." He paused. "Pecos has won the first round," he said grimly, "but there is more to follow.

We had better pick up our prisoner. Come, Hawkins." He turned back to the car and between them they soon had her in running order. Within an hour they were back at the house.

" A queer, out-of-the-way place for me to live in. That's what you're thinking, Hawkins," said Cottle as he led his guest into the house. The prisoner, who was shot through the shoulder, had been bandaged up and put in safe keeping in an out-building, and the car was safely garaged.

" That was just what I was thinking," agreed Billy frankly. " Only how do you know, and how on earth did you know about Pecos when I first met you this afternoon?"

Cottle turned his brilliant blue eyes on Billy. " It's a queer gift I have," he said simply. " When I am looking at a person I can often tell what is in his mind. I can't do it with every one or at all times. But there it is, and it's only fair to tell you."

Billy grinned. " I shall have to be jolly careful what I think about," he said.

" You needn't worry," Cottle told him. " I'm quite accustomed to know that people are thinking odd things about me. But you are tired. Come up, and I'll show you your room."

The house was surprisingly comfortable, and the room into which Cottle took his guest was large and airy and brilliant with electric light. A complete change of clothes lay ready on the bed and there was a bathroom adjoining with plenty of hot water.

Cottle left Billy to change, telling him to come

down as soon as he was ready, and Billy wasted no time about his toilet. He found his host in the dining-room, a handsome room with good prints on the walls, and fine Eastern rugs on the polished floor.

Supper was served by the man named Holmes. " Women won't stay here," explained Cottle. " I have four men and they run everything."

" They can cook, anyhow," said Billy as he was helped to an excellent omelette.

Cottle laughed. " You were thinking I do myself well. Why not? I am well off. I like nice things and I can certainly work better if I am properly fed and looked after."

It was as good a meal as Billy had ever sat down to. Afterwards, excellent coffee was served.

Cottle got up. " Yes," he said, " we will go and look at them."

Billy jumped. " I didn't say anything," he replied quite sharply.

" No, but you are thinking of Pecos' baggage and wondering what is in it."

" I am," confessed Billy; " but all the same, you gave me another shock."

Cottle smiled and led the way to a small room with an iron door which he unlocked with a peculiar key. Pecos' heavy case lay on the floor. Cottle made very short work of the locks, and presently flung the lid back. The first thing he lifted out was a rifle barrel, the next a quantity of heavy blued steel.

" A machine-gun!" exclaimed Billy.

"Just so. One of the Madsen type." As he spoke he was fitting it together. His long fingers were extraordinary deft. He looked up with a frown. "The swine. This is for use against Tenorio."

"Who's he?" asked Billy; "if I may ask," he added apologetically.

"I was going to tell you. Tenorio is the President of the Republic of San Lucar. You know of it?"

"Yes, it is in South America," replied Billy.

"Just so. And Tenorio is a white man. Incidentally, he is a friend of mine. For some years past he has been running San Lucar very comfortably, but about twelve months ago oil was found in San Lucar at a place called Tobosa. The very first bore proved a gusher and the oil is of the finest quality.

"I needn't tell you that in the present state of the world's oil hunger there are millions in it. Tenorio did the right thing and offered the concession to a big British firm on a fifty-fifty basis. San Lucar was to have half of all the profits and he reckoned to use the money for the good of the State, for building railways, schools and bringing everything properly up to date.

"But in any South American State there is always a party out for loot, and in San Lucar their head is a particular poisonous person called Luis Castro. From the moment that the oil was discovered Castro's one idea has been to make himself president, and to get rid of Tenorio.

"If he succeeds he will simply pouch the

whole profits of the oil for a term of years then, when his pockets are full, clear out and live in luxury in Paris for the rest of his life. And Pecos, I may mention, is his jackal.''

Billy nodded. '' I'm getting the hang of it now, sir,'' he said. '' Then I take it that Castro sent Pecos over here to collect the latest in war material for the purpose of scuppering Tenorio.''

'' You've hit it at once. That is the plan of campaign. He is aware that the ordinary South American revolution, a lot of bad shooting and worse swearing, is no go in this case, so he means to wage war with modern methods—planes, bombs, poison gas and the latest in machine-guns.''

'' That's why he was so keen to get hold of the Dolphin,'' said Billy and fell silent, a thoughtful frown puckering his forehead. '' But look here, sir,'' he went on. '' All this sort of thing costs money. Even if they'd managed to steal the Dolphin, one plane is no good. They'd have to build more. It looks to me as if this Castro fellow must have a good deal of cash at his command. Where does he get it?''

'' I was hoping you would ask me that question, Hawkins,'' said the other. '' It tells me that you have your head properly screwed on. Yes, Castro has money at his command, and that is exactly what makes him so dangerous. See here.''

He unlocked a safe and from it took a button of metal which he handed to Billy. '' What do you make of that?'' he asked.

Billy weighed it in his hand, then held it up to the light. "Gold," he said; "but it's green stuff. What makes it so green?"

"That is exactly what I have been trying to find out, and I suspect the presence of an unknown element. This gold, Hawkins, was sent to me by President Tenorio, and he has proof that it came from Castro himself."

He paused for a moment and went on again in a slow, measured tone. "In all the world, so far as I can ascertain, there is only one other specimen of gold which resembles this. That is in the Smithsonian Museum in the States, and it was dug from the ruins of a city in Northern Brazil. It has never been analyzed but it is believed to be the oldest piece of refined gold in existence."

"Northern Brazil—do you mean Bahia?" asked Billy quickly.

"I do."

"And San Lucar borders on Bahia," exclaimed Billy. "I say, sir, is this Atlantean gold?"

Cottle nodded gravely. "That is my conviction," he answered.

"Then Castro has got hold of some ancient hoard, and is using it as the sinews of war," said Billy eagerly. "What a darned shame!"

"Worse than a shame. A sin, Hawkins. I mean to stop it if it is humanly possible, and I want help. No, you need not answer. I knew at once that you would come."

"Come! You bet I'll come, sir," cried Billy.

At that moment a telephone bell rang, and Cottle stepped across the room and put the receiver to his ear. " Yes, Croker, what is it?" he asked. " Yes—all right. I'll be there in a minute," he said, and rang off.

His eyes were all alight as he turned to Billy. " Trouble, Hawkins. Croker telephones from the gate that there are suspicious movements in the fog outside."

CHAPTER FOUR

THE BOMB

BILLY jumped to his feet. " More of them?" he exclaimed.

" The gang," said Cottle, who had stepped across to a cabinet which he unlocked and from which he took a box similar to those in which tennis balls are kept. " No, there is no great hurry," he continued. " Croker is quite capable of guarding the gate."

" But the fog," put in Billy anxiously. " It's thick as soup. Won't it give them a chance of getting up to the gate unseen?"

" Fogs are frequent here," replied Cottle calmly. " So I have taken precautions accordingly." He tucked the box carefully under his arm and led the way from the room and so out of the house. As Billy had said, the fog was thick as soup. The darkness was intense. From the direction of the gate came an occasional deep, low growl.

"Bouncer knows there's something wrong," said Cottle. "I wonder how many there are of the fellows."

"But who are they, sir?" asked Billy. "Surely Pecos and his pals are not back here?"

Cottle laughed softly. "Hardly. Pecos has much more respect for his skin than to tackle me in this fashion. No; these fellows are a bunch of gunmen whom he and Castro have hired to do me in. Unluckily Castro knows that I am the one lion in his path, and is aware that if he could scupper me he would have practically a free hand. I fancy he has put a pretty heavy price on my head."

"You don't let it worry you a lot," said Billy.

"Care killed a cat," smiled Cottle.

It flashed through Billy's mind that in any sort of trouble he would much sooner be on Cottle's side than against him. Yet he could not help feeling a trifle anxious. There were but six men, including Cottle and himself, to guard this considerable enclosure and, young as he was, Billy knew enough of the desperate brutality of these gangs of gunmen—the evil dregs of the slums—to feel that the danger was serious.

They reached the gate, and there was big Croker in his little refuge with a telephone to one ear. "Where are they, Croker?" asked the Professor.

"I can't rightly make out, sir," replied Croker. "I called you up when they crossed the

36

outer wire, and by the microphone I reckoned there was a round dozen of 'em. But they ain't come near the gate and I can't exactly make out which way they've gone."

" Better switch on the lights," said Cottle quietly and his hand went to the switchboard. Next instant a powerful searchlight blazed out. Its ray was of a curious green-blue, and to Billy's astonishment pierced the fog, making the path and the surrounding moor almost as bright as day. Working a lever, Cottle swivelled the light so that the glare swung slowly to and fro in a wide arc. But all that showed was grass and rocks and heather. " Nothing doing," he said. " They've gone round to the back, I suppose."

" That's it, sir," said Croker. " They're going to tackle the garden wall." He chuckled. " They don't know what's awaiting 'em," he added.

Cottle turned swiftly. " Stay here, Croker. Phone Holmes to watch the south wall. Hawkins, take this lantern and come with me."

" You're all wired, I suppose, sir?" said Billy as he took the heavy lantern which Cottle handed him.

" We are wired all right," replied Cottle, " and there are one or two other little traps for the unwary. Still, it never does to underestimate one's opponents, and we have too much at stake to take chances. There's your plane, for one thing, to say nothing of Pecos' machine-gun."

" That gun might come in handy," suggested Billy.

"I have plenty of firearms," said Cottle; "but I doubt if they'll give us a chance to use them. Hallo, what's that?"

Something came hissing through the air to drop on the ground in a potato bed some thirty paces away and at once to burst into brilliant flame.

"A flare! Down quickly, Hawkins," snapped Cottle as he dropped behind a small shrub. Next instant came a spatter of heavy firing and bullets whizzed overhead while a sharp crackle of breaking glass proved that the firing was directed against the house.

"That's a new dodge," said Cottle in Billy's ear. "They must have got a leader who knows his job. He's put his marksmen on stilts or else brought a portable ladder; they are firing from above the level of the wall."

"And we can't stop them," grumbled Billy.

"Never mind; they'll break some glass but that's about all the harm they'll do. And the flare won't burn for long."

Cottle was right, and in any case the flare being only magnesium failed to pierce the fog or even give the attackers any clear vision of the buildings. Next moment it was out, and the firing ceased.

"They haven't got much change out of that," said Cottle. "I wish I knew just where they were. I've a machine-gun on top of the house which would give them beans if I set it going."

"Let's go and try it, sir," said Billy eagerly. "The next flare they throw might give them away."

Cottle hesitated. "Better wait a while. If they caught sight of us they might get us before we reached cover."

All was quiet, so quiet that Billy could actually hear his own heart beating. Yet Cottle close beside him was breathing as evenly as a child asleep.

"He's a big man," said Billy to himself. "And I'm jolly lucky to have fallen in with him. If we get through to-night I certainly shan't have to complain of dullness."

Billy's reflections were suddenly and rudely broken by a tremendous explosion. A huge flash of crimson flame burst luridly through the grey fog and the crash made Billy's ears ring.

"Jumping Jiminy, what's up?" he gasped, and sprang to his feet.

Cottle jumped up too. "They've bombed the wall," he remarked. "I rather thought they were up to some game of that kind. And luckily I prepared for it. Wait here; I'll settle with them." The explosion had occurred almost opposite the place where the two had been lying, and as the darkness shut down after the great burst of flame it was like pitch. Into it Cottle vanished like a ghost, leaving Billy in a very upset state of mind.

What Cottle was up to he had not the faintest idea. Billy did not think he was armed for the only thing he was carrying was that box of tennis balls.

Billy, however, had hardly time to get scared before the Professor's tall form came speeding

back out of the fog. " I timed it exactly right,"
he said as gleefully as a boy. " I thought they'd
be sure to hang back a minute or two so as to
make sure their bomb had done its full work.
It has, too. There's room for a horse and cart to
drive through the wall."

" Then what are we going to do?" gasped
Billy.

Cottle paused a moment before answering.
" Sit tight," he replied.

Billy heard a hoarse voice by the wall, then
a rush of feet. " Here they come!" he said
hoarsely. " And we haven't even a gun."

" Don't worry," Cottle bade him. " You'll
hear something in about two ticks, more or less.
Listen now!"

Billy listened with straining ears. Men were
running forward; he could plainly hear the thud
of heavy boots on the soft earth. Then came a
crackling sound as if someone had trodden on
glass. He heard the amazing Cottle chuckle
softly.

There came a yell, then a second which was
more a shriek than a yell, and this was followed
by gasps and screams as of men suddenly
stricken with some awful plague. There were
crashes and thuds.

" What have you done to them?" gasped
Billy.

" Don't get excited, Hawkins. I haven't
killed them or even done them any lasting
harm," said the Professor quietly. " Come with
40

me and I will show you what happens to tres-
passers on my domain."

He strode off and Billy followed. The noise
was terrific, but since the Professor had not yet
turned on his lantern Billy could not see what
was happening. A man came running out of the
gloom. Billy had to jump back out of his way,
or he would have been knocked down. "Great
ghost! He's crazy!" he exclaimed, and really
it looked as if he were right, for the fellow, a
great, hefty-looking ruffian, was tearing off his
clothes as he ran and shrieking like a lunatic.

Cottle switched on his light. In an instant the
whole surroundings leaped out. There was the
gap in the wall, big enough, as Cottle had said,
to drive a cart through it, and there was the
garden with its potatoes and cabbages. The beds
looked as if a herd of buffaloes had been stam-
peded over them, and about a dozen most evil-
looking toughs were dancing and stamping
about, all like the first, busily engaged in tearing
off their clothes.

"Don't go too close," said Cottle warningly
to Billy. "I don't want to see you start un-
dressing."

"For any sake, what does it mean?"
demanded Billy.

"I'll explain later. For the moment our job
is to round-up these beauties." He whistled
shrilly as he spoke and Holmes and his other
house-man came running up. Each carried a
short-barrelled shotgun. "Now then, you
beauties," shouted Cottle in a voice that rang

like a trumpet blast, " if you've quite finished dancing on my vegetables perhaps you'll kindly accompany me to the house."

The men paid no attention whatever. The nearest, stripped to the waist, was tearing at his flesh with his fingernails. Cottle collared him roughly. " Stop that, you fool! " he ordered sharply.

" I can't. I'm stung all over," groaned the wretched man.

" You're not. It's only gas. March, and I'll soon fix you up. Here, Holmes, put a pair of cuffs on him."

Holmes promptly handcuffed the fellow and then a second, and dragged them off. The men made no attempt at resistance. In a very short time the whole lot were secured.

" Take 'em into the old laboratory," ordered Cottle, and they were led into a large, shed-like place. The Professor took a jar from a shelf, poured its contents into a basin, and flung in four or five small sponges. " Strip them and rub them down," he directed, and this was done. The results were almost magical. The prisoners' skins, which had all been red and inflamed, at once lost their angry colour, and the prisoners themselves calmed down.

" No, we won't take your handcuffs off," said Cottle grimly. " You can stick here for a bit and think what fools you've made of yourselves, tackling me with bombs and rifles. I'll wager something considerable you don't try it again."

"What are you going to do with us?" demanded one of them sullenly.

"What were you going to do with me?" retorted Cottle.

The man, a bullet-headed fellow with a blue-black jowl and eyes like black shoe buttons, was silent.

"So you've nothing to say," said Cottle. "You're not going to confess that you were paid to murder me, for you think that if you did I might retort in kind. Well, you've had a sample of my power, and I'll tell you this, that, if you attempt to play the fool, the next thing that will happen will make this look like a flea bite."

With which threat he marched off, and, switching off the light, locked and barred the door behind him.

Billy kept silent until he and his host were back in the warm, well-lighted study. Cottle looked at him and laughed. "Good for you, Hawkins! You never turned a hair. And now I'll reward by answering the questions that are trembling on your lips.

"It was simple enough. That box was full of small glass balls, each charged with a certain gas which I invented some little time ago. I call it sting gas. As soon as those beauties came trampling over the containers it rose all over them, and you saw for yourself what it did. It makes the sufferer feel as if a million mosquitoes had bitten him at once. I got a dose of it myself on one occasion, so I know."

"It licks mustard gas into a cocked hat,"

43

declared Billy. " Why, you could rout an army corps with a few hundred of those patents!"

Cottle nodded. " It may be useful. I shall take some out with me. And now, after all that excitement, what price bed?"

" I am a bit sleepy, I'll admit," agreed Billy. " But first, I wish you'd tell me what you mean to do with that bunch of hoboes."

" Turn 'em over to the police," replied Cottle. " It's a nuisance, for it means delay, but it wouldn't be straight good to let 'em go. I shall get on to the police station at Tarnmouth at once, and ask them to send up a force and a couple of cars first thing in the morning." He got up and offered Billy his hand. " Good-night, Hawkins. I congratulate myself on having a useful ally."

Billy's eyes shone. " And I'm just hugging myself, sir, at the prospect of what's before us." He laughed. " Only to think of it. Less than twelve hours ago I was grousing to Len Holton about being bored stiff.

Cottle's bright blue eyes twinkled. " Boredom is a complaint from which you are not likely to suffer in the immediate future. I can promise you that, Hawkins."

COTTLE COVETS A PLANE

WEARY after his exciting day, Billy slept like a dormouse until roused by Holmes who brought a cup of tea and a couple of slices of delicately cut bread and butter.

" Prisoners all right, Holmes?" was his first question.

" I reckon so, sir," replied Holmes with a twinkle in his eyes. " They left here a matter of two hours ago under escort of a sergeant and six bluebottles."

It was a gorgeous morning. The fog had all gone and the moorland air was like crystal for clearness. As Billy leaped out of bed and set about his toilet his face was as bright as the morning. What luck! What gorgeous and wonderful luck was his! At that moment he had no hard thoughts towards that rascal Juan Pecos himself, for, like Kipling's hero, Billy was going to " buy a 'am an' see life."

As Holmes had promised, breakfast was waiting, and, like supper the previous evening, was a meal fit for epicures. Having absorbed two exquisitely fresh eggs, a plate of finely sliced, home-cured bacon, sundry pieces of toast with honey, and several cups of fragrant coffee, Billy felt ready for anything that might betide.

Then he and the Professor talked. " I've got

take the plane back to Marchester, sir," said Billy.

" Will you give me a lift?" asked Cottle.

" Sure!" said Billy. " But——"

" But what do I want in Marchester? you were going to ask. I don't want anything there, but I want to go to London, and Marchester is only two hours from Town by the twelve o'clock express whereas here I am nearly six hours."

" I understand, sir. Barring accidents, I'll have you in Marchester by eleven."

" I'll be ready in ten minutes. Meantime, you had better write out an application to resign your commission and I will present it when I reach Town."

He laughed as he saw Billy's eyes widen. " Yes, I have a bit of a pull with the bigwigs," he added, " and I want you out as quick as can be. We must sail within a week."

Billy gasped. Accustomed as he was to Army red tape, he could not believe that things could be done so quickly. But as he realized that the Professor was in earnest he hurried out to get the plane ready. Holmes helped, and inside the agreed ten minutes her tank was full and all prepared.

Cottle took his seat, the big machine rose and climbed steeply into the blue, sun-washed sky.

Green England reeled away beneath her like a cinema film.

Cottle was enchanted. " I've done a bit of flying, but this beats all," he told Billy. " I've never known anything like it."

By half-past ten the smoke cloud above Manchester lay on the northern horizon and exactly at a quarter to eleven Billy brought the Dolphin to rest on the aerodrome. Cottle jumped out and walked round the machine, taking in every detail with those brilliant eyes of his. " I don't wonder Pecos wanted her," he told Billy. " So do I, and, by thunder, I'm going to have her."

" You can't, sir," said Billy. " She's for the Government—worse luck!"

" I tell you I'm going to have her," declared Cottle. " With this machine I can run rings round Castro."

Len Holton had come up and Billy introduced him. " Professor Cottle says he's going to make off with your Dolphin," he grinned.

" And I'm going to have Hawkins as my pilot," remarked Cottle. " I suppose he hasn't yet told you how he saved your machine for you yesterday."

Len opened his eyes. " Not a word," he said.

" Then I'll tell you," said Cottle.

When he had finished, Len turned to Billy. " You lucky beggar!" he exclaimed enviously. " And only yesterday you were grousing about the dullness of life. But this is a wonderful stunt. And, as the Professor says, a really top-hole plane would be worth a lot in such a show."

" It's the Dolphin I want," said Cottle. " See here, Mr. Holton, if I pay their price and square it with the Powers in London can I have her?"

" Oh, so far as the firm is concerned, I could promise that, sir, but you'll strike a snag when

47

you tackle H.Q. By the by, Sir Francis Wing is staying at Molton Hall not ten miles from here. He's the Lord High Muck-a-Muck in air matters. Why don't you flip over and see him?''

'' The very thing!'' exclaimed Cottle. '' May Billy take me in the Dolphin?''

'' Mr. Webster is somewhere around,'' said Len. '' I'll see him.''

He hurried off and presently came back with Mr. Webster himself in tow. The chief partner had, of course, heard of Cottle and was very cordial. He readily gave permission and said he would telephone Sir Francis to ask him if he could see the Professor.

He came back presently with word that Sir Francis would be pleased to see Professor Cottle at luncheon, and a little later Billy and his new employer were again in the air.

Molton Hall was the home of Lord Marchester, who, like Sir Francis, was a member of the Cabinet. He was a solid, square-built man going rather bald, a complete contrast to Sir Francis Wing the Air Minister, who was as tall as Cottle, had a face like an eagle and eyes the colour of steel.

The cordial way in which they both welcomed Cottle was an eye-opener for Billy, but when the Professor put forward his request to be allowed to purchase the Dolphin Sir Francis shook his head.

'' Very sorry, Professor, but it can't be done. We couldn't risk a machine like that leaving

England. Supposing it fell into the hands of a foreign Power?"

"Exactly what it would have done yesterday but for young Hawkins here, Sir Francis," answered Cottle.

"Tell us," said Sir Francis, and again Billy had to listen to the story of his doings on the previous day.

Sir Francis looked at him very kindly. "You do us credit, Hawkins," he said so cordially that Billy crimsoned. "Jove, I'd like to have seen the face of this dago gentleman when you started stunting."

"It was a bit green, sir," allowed Billy, and they all laughed.

Sir Francis turned to Cottle. "I should like to see you snooker this Castro person," he said. "And I'll see that you have a really good machine to take out. If you want Hawkins, why, he shall have leave for the necessary period. I don't want to lose him from the Force."

"It's awfully kind of you, sir," faltered Billy.

Sir Francis smiled. "Come into the house, you and the Professor. Lunch will be ready in about an hour. Meantime, Lord Marchester and I have a certain matter to talk over, so you must excuse us."

Cottle and Billy were left to amuse themselves in the billiard room. "I'm pretty sure I know what's up," Cottle told him. "It's the French business. There's a new treaty on the stocks, and Sir Francis has come up here with a rough draft to show Marchester."

Billy was not much interested, for he was thinking far more of San Lucar than of France. " It's a pity we can't have the Dolphin, sir," he said.

" I haven't given up hope yet," replied the other. " Now I'll play you a hundred up before lunch."

The game was about half-way through when the door was burst open and Sir Francis hurried in. His handsome face was set like stone, but his eyes betrayed a terrible excitement. Behind him was Lord Marchester, his usually ruddy face pale as death.

" Something very serious has happened," said Sir Francis, addressing Cottle. " Papers of extreme importance have disappeared."

Billy spoke up. " I heard a car pass down the drive a few minutes ago."

" A car!" exclaimed Sir Francis and darted out. Billy raced alongside and together they reached the front door. " My own!" gasped Sir Francis. " It must have been that man who posed as a Foreign Office messenger. And we have nothing to catch him."

" What about the plane, sir? The Dolphin will catch most things," said Billy. Without waiting for an answer he started running for the spot where he had left the plane.

The plane was in the park, only a few hundred yards from the house but hidden by trees, and Billy simply raced for it. He had a horrid fear that this spy person might have had the idea of putting her out of action before making his escape. But either the man had not had time, or the idea had not occurred to him, and with a sigh of relief Billy saw that all was well.

Quick as he had been, Sir Francis was alongside him and the two reached the Dolphin together. " They are Lord Marchester's manuscript notes," explained Sir Francis. " Notes for the new agreement between France and this country. They were left on the table for a few minutes while I was speaking at the telephone in the next room, and this man, whom we both believed to be Gage, one of the Foreign Office messengers, managed to get away with them, leaving an empty envelope in their stead. Hawkins, this spy must be stopped at all costs, for if the notes got into the wrong hands the consequences will be serious."

Billy nodded. " Any notion which way he will go, sir?" he asked.

" East. The chances are he has a plane somewhere not very far off."

The words were hardly out of his mouth before the heavy clatter of an aeroplane engine broke the warm silence. " There he is, sir," cried Billy, pointing to a dark object rising beyond a wood about two miles away to the eastward. " All right. I'll get him."

Lord Marchester came panting up, accompanied by Cottle. " There he goes!" he exclaimed. " Wing, I shall phone to Headquarters to send an Air Force plane after him. We must stop him at any price."

" Not a bit of use," snapped Sir Francis. " He'd be a hundred miles away before they got started. Hawkins and I will tackle this job." As he spoke he was already in the passenger's seat behind Billy.

" You are coming, sir?" exclaimed Billy in amazement.

" Of course I'm coming. How are you for petrol?"

" Tanks full, sir. Good for five hundred miles."

" Thanks be for that. Let her go."

The self-starter buzzed, the great engine roared and the big machine rolled swiftly across the turf. " Good-bye, Billy. Good luck!" shouted Cottle. Then the Dolphin lifted and in a matter of seconds was climbing steeply.

Sir Francis spoke in Billy's ear. " Give her all she'll take, Hawkins," he said, and Billy felt, rather than heard, the intense earnestness behind the words. " That is one of the new Stellens, and said to be good for two hundred and sixty."

" Then we have our work cut out, sir," replied Billy; " but I think we shall be all right. I've never yet flown anything to beat this bus."

Cheerfully as Billy spoke, inwardly he was anything but happy. The Stellen he had never before seen, but had heard much of her extraordinary speed. And the worst of it was that she had a start of at least five miles. He reached the three-thousand foot level, flattened out and set himself to get every ounce of power possible out of the Dolphin. She responded nobly and gradually the needle crept up until it showed a speed of two hundred and sixty.

Billy's eyes were fixed on the chase, but in spite of the tremendous pace at which the Dolphin was travelling she did not seem to gain an inch upon the other plane. The latter was undoubtedly holding the start. The minutes slipped by and at last Sir Francis spoke again. " She has the legs of us, Hawkins," he muttered.

" We've a long way to go, sir," replied Billy consolingly.

" Which means all the more time for the fellow to get away from us," responded Sir Francis, and Billy knew by his tone the terrible strain he was enduring. Some time passed before either spoke again. Then Billy asked a question. " Have you seen the paper this morning, Sir Francis?"

" Yes—why?"

" What was the weather report, sir?"

" Oh, I understand. It was good for the West of England, but spoke of a secondary depression working down into the North Sea."

" I thought as much," said Billy, pointing to a dark line on the horizon straight ahead.

Sir Francis drew a quick breath. " That finishes it, Hawkins. Once the fellow reaches those clouds we lose him."

Billy shook his head. " I don't know so much about that, sir. It means we shall strike a head wind shortly, and that's where this bus scores."

" You think so?"

" I know it," declared Billy. " You'll see."

The tremendous pace at which they travelled made the cloud bank appear to rise like magic. Within a very few minutes the Stellen plunged into it, and vanished from their sight. " Suppose he dodges," was the thought that flashed through Billy's mind. But it was no use supposing, so Billy carried on. The bright sunlight dimmed, then in an instant the Dolphin had rushed into a bank of dense fog.

" I'm going higher, sir," shouted Billy pulling over the control. The fog dimmed, a gleam of light broke through, then suddenly the Dolphin had flashed out into sunlight, and below lay miles of cloud white as fleece in the strong light. Billy's eyes roved the horizon, but there was no sign of anything besides themselves in the vast expanse.

The blue above was laced with lines of cirrus cloud and the hum of the wire stays rose a note higher. The Dolphin was butting into the teeth of a fifty-mile-an-hour gale. Again he pulled over the control and again the nose of the Dolphin tilted upwards. " Got to get above this," he explained to Sir Francis.

The cold grew bitter as the machine climbed higher, but still the gale blew fiercely. The six-thousand-feet level was passed, then the seven, yet still the plane climbed. Then all at once the shrilling of the gale lessened. " Done it!" cried Billy joyfully. " We're above it, sir. What's more, we've the wind with instead of against us."

Sir Francis merely nodded, but a little of the bitter strain passed from his face. Although there was no landmark to judge by Billy felt that the speed had jumped enormously, and knew that the Dolphin must now be travelling far faster than the Stellen. " Watch, please," he asked of his companion. " We don't want to overrun her."

Came a break in the great cloud mass beneath, and Billy had a glimpse of green water a mile and a half below him. But there was no sign of the chase.

" Head for Rotterdam," said Sir Francis. " You may take it that is his line. The words were hardly out of his mouth before Billy gave a cry. " Look! There below us!"

In the murk beneath a shape flashed into sight, a shape like a huge fish shooting through the depths of a great pool.

" The Stellen!" snapped Sir Francis, and even as he spoke Billy had dived straight down upon the half-seen form. So quick was he that he was right on top of the Stellen before her pilot saw him. When he did he ducked and dived like a minnow flying from a pike. Billy plunged again into the fog and gale, and, giving the Dolphin every atom of gas he could take, clung to the tail of the chase.

A spurt of flame flashed from the Stellen. Bullets ripped through the wing just above Billy's head and he saw Sir Francis draw a heavy pistol from his coat pocket. " Hold on, sir!" he shouted. " I'll get above him."

The Dolphin responded marvellously. She was built for that sort of thing. She rose swiftly. The man in the Stellen fired again and again, but he was shooting wildly. Another moment and the Dolphin was exactly above the other plane. Billy got a glimpse of her pilot staring up with horror-stricken face, then Sir Francis, leaning over, deliberately emptied his revolver into the Stellen. Her pilot crumpled in his seat and his machine, uncontrolled, shot suddenly upwards. So suddenly that it took all Billy's skill to avoid being rammed.

For a moment his eyes were off her. He heard Sir Francis shout, then, when he was able to look back, he saw the Stellen rolling over and over, toppling helplessly through the fog towards the unseen sea beneath.

Sir Francis drew a long, whistling breath. "Saved!" he said hoarsely. Then, after a pause: "Get home, Hawkins."

CHAPTER SIX

GREEN GOLD

BILLY came into the Professor's big workroom with a number of letters. " Post in, sir," he said rather breathlessly. " And—and a letter from Sir Francis."

Cottle took it, ripped it open, and began to read. Billy, watching, saw his blue eyes gleam. " It's all right, Billy!"

" You mean you've got the plane?" cried Billy.

" Not I," replied Cottle. " It was your doing entirely."

Billy gave a whoop of delight. " So long as it's ours, nothing else matters," he declared. " I'm awfully glad, sir. Now we can really start."

" Yes. Sir Francis says that the Dolphin will be packed for shipment by the *Clumber Castle*. We leave to-morrow, Billy."

" I'm packed, sir," said Billy, but Cottle was reading another letter. " This is from Lord Marchester," he said. " He told me the other day that there was one man in England who could probably tell me something useful about the green gold. He is Colonel Parton, R.E., the South American explorer. Lord Marchester says he has written to him and asked him to look me up. He may be here to-day."

" That sounds interesting," said Billy, and, as he spoke, the telephone from the lodge rang and Billy took off the receiver. " He's here, sir," he told Cottle. " Colonel Parton is at the gate."

" Good business! Bring him in, Billy."

A car was at the gate, and in it sat a man with a face so sunburned that to Billy he looked like a half-breed. He was about fifty, but though his hair was going grey he seemed hard as nails and tough as shoe leather.

" I am Colonel Parton," he said. " Is Professor Cottle at home?"

" Yes, sir, and expecting you," Billy answered. " Come in."

The Colonel glanced at the walls and the well-defended gate. " The place looks as though it was built to stand a siege," he said.

" There's a good deal of value inside," Billy explained. " This way, sir."

Cottle was waiting in the sitting-room. As he stepped forward Billy saw that his brilliant eyes took in every detail of the visitor's appearance. " Very good of you to come all this way, Colonel Parton," he said courteously.

" Not at all, Professor," answered the other. " This gold of which Lord Marchester spoke interests me."

" Here is a sample," said Cottle, handing over a fragment of the greenish-yellow metal similar to what Billy had previously seen. " I should be very glad if you could give me any idea where it comes from."

Colonel Parton took it to the window and examined it in the light. " Yes," he said. " I have seen some of this before. It is without doubt Atlantean Gold."

" I think I knew that," said Cottle civilly. " What I am most anxious to ascertain is where it comes from."

" Parral," replied the other at once.

" The Southern province?" questioned Cottle, his eyes fixed on the Colonel.

" Yes. That is my opinion. There is a ruined city which lies in the centre of great swamps beyond the Maranao Mountains. From Indians who have visited it I obtained gold similar to this specimen. The gold is, of course, pre-Aztec."

" Thank you very much, Colonel," said Cottle. " Your information is of the greatest value. May I offer you some luncheon?"

" I thank you," replied Colonel Parton formally, " but I am due at Exeter by four, and, with your permission, will be pushing on at once."

" I am sorry," said Cottle. " Hawkins, will you see our visitor to the gate?"

When Billy came back he found Cottle chuckling consumedly.

" What's the matter, sir?" he asked.

" He did it well, didn't he?" laughed Cottle.

" What on earth do you mean, sir?" asked Billy, bewildered.

" Our visitor, of course. The self-styled Colonel Parton."

" Self-styled?" repeated Billy, utterly puzzled.

" You mean to say that he was not Colonel Parton?"

" I am quite sure he was nothing of the sort, though I must say his disguise was good."

" But how do you know?" demanded Billy.

" Because I happen to have heard the real Colonel Parton lecture. It's easy enough to make up to resemble another man, but it's quite another thing to imitate his voice. The moment our visitor opened his mouth I knew he was a fraud."

Billy stared. " But what was his object?" he asked.

" Don't be dense, Billy. It was simply to put us off the track."

" But you said you were obliged for his information?"

" So I am, for, since he told me that the place from which the gold comes is the Southern province, you may take it as certain that the real direction is the opposite. He has gone away under the impression that he has humbugged me completely, and now his employers will take it for granted that, if we reach San Lucar, we shall go cruising away down into Parral."

" If we reach San Lucar?" repeated Billy. " Do you mean that they will have another try at stopping us?"

" I am very sure they will," answered Cottle grimly. " You see, Billy, I know my Castro."

Billy stood frowning thoughtfully. " But what about the real Colonel Parton?" he asked. " How could this sham fellow know that the real one would not turn up and put us wise to the substitution?"

Cottle shook his head. "That I don't know, Billy, but you may take it that Castro's man, before he came, made sure that the real man was not coming. Probably he sent him a forged letter in my name."

"Phew, but this is a cheery crowd we're up against!" exclaimed Billy.

Cottle laughed. "You'll know more about that before we're finished," he said. "And now to our packing."

Billy stood at the rail of the *Clumber Castle*, anxiously watching the landing-stage, and every now and then glancing at his wrist-watch. The baggage, including the plane, was all aboard, and in five minutes the ship was due to sail.

But Cottle was not yet aboard. He had sent Billy on with their luggage early in the afternoon, telling him that he had a few odds and ends to buy and that he would join him later. The seconds ticked by and still there was no sign of Cottle. Once more Billy looked at his watch. It was now three minutes to four, and four was the hour for sailing. The last visitors were already leaving the ship, and men were ready at the gangways to raise them.

One minute left and all the gangways but one had been removed. The men were at the ropes of the last when a taxi came into sight, driving furiously. "Wait!" shouted Billy to the men at the gangway. "Here's a passenger."

As the taxi came shooting up another came into sight, travelling even faster than the first. The first pulled up with a screech of brakes, the door flung open and Cottle leapt out. He flung a note to the driver, then raced for the gangway. As his feet touched the deck the gangway lifted off the stage. "Jove, that was a close call!" gasped Billy.

"I meant it to be," replied the Professor. "Watch!"

The second taxi had discharged a squat, brown-faced man with bristling black hair who made a dart for the gangway. He was too late. The shore end was already the height of his head above the wharf. "Let her down!" he shrieked shrilly. "I weesh to come aboard."

"Sorry! It's too late, sir," replied the man in charge. "Afraid you'll have to wait for the next boat."

The brown-faced man burst into a torrent of language which, luckily perhaps for him, was not English, though even so the dock policeman moved nearer. Then quite suddenly the fellow turned and dashed back into his taxi, slammed the door, and was driven away.

"Another of 'em?" said Billy to Cottle.

"Another of them," Cottle answered. "I made up my mind that one of the gang would be told off to accompany us on the voyage, and it seemed to me that my only chance to dodge him was to wait like this until the last minute."

"You certainly cut it fine," said Billy, watching the widening gap between the ship and the shore. " All the same, I don't quite see how it worked."

" Surely it's plain enough. I knew I was being shadowed, but the fellow was too clever to let me identify him. So I had to humbug him into thinking that I was going to miss the boat. Ten minutes ago his nerves got the better of him and he showed up. Of course, I had a taxi waiting round the corner, but, unluckily for himself, our friend had neglected to take a similar precaution." He stopped with a smile.

Billy nodded.

" You gave me a horrid scare, but I see now it was worth it. We shall have a nice peaceful voyage."

" I hope so," replied Cottle.

The weather was delightful, the passengers were pleasant, and Billy enjoyed himself greatly. Cottle let him do pretty much as he liked, except that for two hours in the day he made him work at Spanish.

Day by day as they drove south-west the weather grew warmer, but Cottle had secured a deck cabin for Billy and himself and, although below it was sweltering, on deck the breeze caused by the ship's motion made the heat bearable. As they neared the Equator they struck thundery weather and Billy had never seen such lightning.

One afternoon he and Cottle stood together leaning on the rail. A storm had passed over, but now the sky was clearing and there was a pleasant breeze.

" Getting pretty close, aren't we, sir?" said Billy.

" Yes. We ought to sight land to-morrow," replied the other. " Then work begins," he added rather grimly.

" I'm quite ready for it, sir," replied Billy quietly. As he spoke a man came out of the door of the wireless room and ran to the bridge. " What's the hurry, I wonder?" asked Billy in surprise.

Cottle was watching the bridge. " An S O S, I believe," he said quickly. " Yes," said Cottle presently, " I was right. See! We are changing course." He walked aft and Billy followed. As they reached the bridge they met Captain Gaunt, the skipper, coming down."

" Changed course, I see, Captain," remarked Cottle.

" You see too much, Professor," replied Gaunt with a rather wry smile. " Yes, some fool has piled himself up Cape Catuba and is shrieking for help. I have to go fifty miles out of my way to see what the trouble is."

" Interesting," repeated Cottle. " I've never seen a rescue at sea."

" All right, only don't tell any one else," said Gaunt. Cottle nodded and he and Billy went back forward.

It was deliciously cool after the blazing morning, and the *Clumber Castle* drove rapidly across the calm sea. It was still daylight when Cottle pointed to a shadowy cloud against the horizon. " There's Cape Catuba," he said.

In contrast to the low sandy shores of North America the Atlantic coast of the South American continent, south of the Amazon delta, is bold and rugged. Cape Catuba was a great craggy cliff bounding the north side of a deep, narrow bay resembling a Norwegian fiord.

As the *Clumber Castle* came nearer the land, Cottle, who was using a pair of powerful field-glasses, lowered them and turned to Billy. He seemed puzzled. " I can see the ship," he said, " and she is hard and fast on a rock, but I can't see a soul aboard her. There's something fishy about this. I'm going to speak to Gaunt."

At that moment the Captain came up. The decks were comparatively empty, for the passengers, who knew nothing of the change of course, were at dinner. " There's no one aboard, skipper," said Cottle. " And what's that plane doing?" As he spoke a plane had come into sight flying over the stranded ship. It flew out towards the liner, turned and disappeared down the fiord.

" Blessed if I know what they're playing at," growled Gaunt. " Anyhow, I'm not risking my ship near those reefs. I shall stand by and send in a boat." He gave orders, the engines slowed and the big ship lay motionless while a boat was lowered. The sun had set, the swift tropical dusk was settling over the sea and the outlines of the stranded vessel became hazy.

The ship's boat was about half-way to the wreck when the silence was broken by a clatter resembling that of an aeroplane engine. Next instant something shot out from behind the wreck and came tearing across the sea in the direction of the ship.

"A launch!" exclaimed Billy. "And, by gum, she's a big 'un!"

"What does it mean?" demanded the skipper in amazement.

"It means treachery, Captain," replied Cottle quickly. "The whole business is a trap. Your only chance is to clear out as fast as your engines will take you."

"Impossible," returned the other. "I can't abandon my boat."

"Then we must fight," said Cottle.

"Fight—what with? I've a pistol—nothing else."

"Couple up the hosepipes. Give them a dose of steam from the boilers."

"That's a notion," said Gaunt, and sprang to give orders.

"It's no use, sir," said Billy to Cottle. "Look at the pace she's coming. She'll be alongside before we can do a thing."

Cottle saw that Billy was right. The launch was coming like an express train, with a huge wave towering at her stern. "Wait here, Billy," snapped Cottle. "I'm getting something from our cabin."

He dashed down, but before he could get back the launch was alongside. She was a big craft at least fifty feet long, and her decks were crowded with swarthy-looking scoundrels. All were armed, and two heavy machine-guns were fixed

66

in the bows. A man in a sort of uniform sprang forward.

" Where is ze Captain?" he shouted. " I want ze Captain, queek. Eef he not come I sink ze ship."

CHAPTER SEVEN

THE IRON RANSOM

CAPTAIN GAUNT stepped to the rail. " You infernal pirate, what do you mean by talking like this to the Captain of a British vessel?" he demanded. " Who are you?"

The uniformed man snarled like an angry cat. " I weel soon teach you who I am," he retorted. " I will also teach you not to insult a Spanish gentleman. My name is Esteban Garcia, and if I give ze word I blow your ship out of ze water."

Gaunt almost choked with indignation. Billy spoke. " A fat lot of good that will do you, Mr. Garcia," he remarked. " You know darned well what your master, Castro, would say if you did start blowing up the ship. Suppose you say what you really want—that is, if you can talk English enough to tell us."

Garcia's dark face went almost black with fury, his eyes contracted. For a moment he glared at Billy in speechless rage, then suddenly his expression changed to one of triumph. " Eet ees ze fly man, ze boy Hawkins," he exclaimed.

" Yes, I weel tell you what I want. Eet ees you and ze man Cottle. And when I have you Señor Castro he weel give you to me and to Juan Pecos and we weel teach you ze manners."

" You will teach me manners?" Billy's laugh was a worse insult than his words, and for a moment it looked as though the " Spanish gentleman " would have an apoplectic fit.

" Be quiet, Mr. Hawkins," cut in the skipper sternly. " Cannot you see that you are only making matters worse? And it is true, as the scoundrel says, we are absolutely at his mercy."

" Don't be too sure of that. Just remember that Professor Cottle is aboard, Captain," replied Billy in a low voice. " Ah, here he comes."

Cottle came swinging through the group gathered about the rail, his tall figure standing nearly a head above most of them. " Called for us, I suppose, haven't they?" he remarked in his clear, ringing voice.

" Ha, eet ees Cottle!" cried Garcia. " You have right. Eet ees you and ze boy Hawkins zat we demand. Also ze airplane zat you 'ave in ze ship."

" You can demand all right, but you won't get them," roared Gaunt. " You are nothing but a pirate, Mr. Garcia, and let me tell you that piracy is out of date since the war."

Garcia grinned evilly. " 'Ard words, zey break no bones. You 'ave no choice, Captain. We 'ave our guns trained on you, and we 'ave ze bombs." He stooped swiftly and snatched up a small dark object from a rack at his feet. " Eef I throw zat aboard, you all die," he snarled.

Cottle turned to Gaunt. " Let me talk to the pretty gentleman, skipper. I mean it, please. It is through me that you have got into this trouble, and the best I can do is to settle the matter. Do you give me a free hand?"

" I suppose I must," said Gaunt chokingly. " If it was myself I'd tell the coffee-coloured sweep to do his darndest, but I have my passengers to consider."

" I quite understand," said Cottle, and leaned over the rail. " Listen to me, Señor Garcia," he said quietly. " Threats as to throwing bombs cut no ice. It's true that you might kill Hawkins and myself, but you would lose the plane, which, I take it, is what you want most. Now I'm open to a bargain. Will you take the plane and be satisfied with that?"

" No. You weel come wiz me—you, and ze boy Hawkins."

" If we do, do you give your word that our lives will be safe?"

Billy could hardly believe his ears. It was beyond belief that Cottle should make such terms.

Garcia grinned again, and his grin was worse than his scowl. " Yes, I will promise zat you have your lives," he said. " Now I 'ave 'ad enough of talking," he added sharply. " You weel get out ze airplane queek or take ze consequences." He spoke to his men in Spanish, and Billy now knew enough of the language to understand his order. It was that six of them should go aboard the *Clumber Castle* well armed, and see to the hatch being opened. In a moment they came piling over the side, as dirty and dangerous-looking a gang as any one could wish to avoid.

" You see how it is, skipper," said Cottle to Gaunt. " The beggars have the drop on us and we can't help ourselves. You will have to let them take the plane."

Gaunt spoke to the quartermaster and in dry, harsh tones ordered him to open the cargo hatch and start the donkey again. Garcia heard the order, and Billy's fingers itched as he saw the look of triumph on the man's brown face.

" You'll never let them use the Dolphin?" Billy whispered imploringly to Cottle.

" Keep silence," replied Cottle rapidly but in an equally low tone.

Billy resigned himself to silence, but a cold despair was creeping over him.

" You will come aboard ze launch now, Señor Cottle," ordered Garcia.

" If you like," replied Cottle with a shrug, " but if I do there will be no one to check the cases. The aeroplane and its parts are packed in several cases, and Hawkins and myself are the only ones who can identify them. You had better let us stay until the cases are transhipped."

" Zen you can stay," sneered Garcia.

Cottle went meekly over the hatch, and pointed out to the quartermaster in charge a huge case which lay on top of the cargo. " That will be the first," he said tamely.

Two of Garcia's men, each armed with a revolver, stood close to him, and it was evident that the rebel leader, however much he despised the Englishman, was taking no chances. Cottle spoke to one of them in Spanish. "The launch must come close alongside," he said. "Will you tell Señor Garcia?"

"Tell him yourself, gringo," retorted the man roughly. Billy burned to hoof the man overboard, but Cottle showed no sign of resentment at the insult. He obeyed, and with much shouting the launch was moved close under the side of the big steamer. Garcia's ragamuffins, who were on the deck of the *Clumber Castle*, brandished their pistols and forced the rest of the watch who were on deck to keep their distance. The English sailors stood silent and scowling.

The donkey engine began to clank, the chain tightened and a huge square case came slowly up out of the depths below. It was marked in big black letters with Mark Cottle's name. "Hurry! Hurry!" snapped Garcia. "Lazy dogs, do you think I have all night to waste? Hurry, or I will come aboard and make you."

Billy saw a dull-red flush mount to the cheeks of one of the men working the crane, while another clenched his big fists and his eyes gleamed dangerously. Of them all Cottle was the only one who showed no signs of anger or impatience. Billy felt sick with shame.

"We are hurrying all we can, señor," said Cottle in a tone of apology. "But the engine of a great machine like this must be handled carefully.''

'' You weel do some of the handling next time,'' promised Garcia jeeringly. Cottle did not answer, and the case, which had now been raised carefully clear of the deck, was swung steadily outwards until it was exactly over the centre of the afterpart of the launch.

'' Ready!'' cried Cottle. '' Lower away.''

Next instant there was a loud crack from somewhere down in the hold, the wire rope rushed out through the pulleys and the huge case fell bodily upon the launch, striking it with a most appalling crash. The whole stem of the launch crumbled into ruin under the impact, while her bow end leaped upwards with such force as threw Garcia and all those with him flat on the deck.

At the same instant Cottle suddenly came to life and, swinging upon the nearest dago, picked him up bodily and flung him over the rail. With a joyous whoop Billy got hold of another and, first yanking his gun out of his hand, smote him on the jaw so that he lost all interest in the proceedings and lay twitching on the deck.

The watch were not slow to follow this example. Indeed, they were so quick about it that only one of Garcia's blackguards managed to squib off his pistol. No one was hit, and he followed his fellows into the sea.

Garcia was the first of his own lot to recover. With a bound he was on his feet and making for the nearest of his guns. At the same moment Cottle, leaning over the rail, flung something that looked like a black orange down upon the deck of the launch. With a ringing crack it leaped into a sheet of flame, and in an instant the forepart of the launch was all ablaze. The explosion knocked Garcia overboard. As for his men, left without a leader, they one and all lost their heads and leaped into the sea. In a matter of seconds there was not one living man left aboard the sinking, burning craft.

" Push off, Captain!" cried Cottle in his old ringing voice. " Push off or she'll scorch your paint."

Billy leaped forward. " The engine. We must save the engine."

Cottle laughed. " Keep your wool on, Billy. It's only pig iron."

Billy gazed at the other in amazement. " You—you didn't expect this?" he gasped.

Cottle laughed again. " What do you think?" he chuckled.

At that moment the twin screws began to revolve and the big ship drew away from the sinking bonfire.

Ten minutes later she had picked up her boat, and was steaming steadily away across the calm sea to her original destination.

Cottle stood gazing at the red glow which still showed near the island. " First trick to us, Billy, but don't be too bucked. Castro is a very much tougher meat than either Pecos or the late Mr. Garcia.

.   .   .   .   .

Even in England the Professor, with his great

73

height, his keen face and flashing blue eyes, had been a notable figure, but in Las Cruces, the capital of San Lucar, he created a positive sensation. As Billy and he walked along the shady side of the blazing street every one turned to stare at the two Englishmen. And Billy, glancing up at the splendid figure of his companion, did not wonder.

They were on their way to call on the President, and for this occasion Cottle had got up in a suit of snow-white drill. He wore white buckskin shoes, a Panama hat and a blue silk tie, and looked magnificent.

The President was waiting for them. Tenorio was a very different-looking man from most of the inhabitants of his little republic, for he was nearly as tall as Cottle and as fair as Billy.

There was no doubt about the President's delight at seeing Cottle. He took both his hands and shook them eagerly. " I cannot tell you how glad I am to see you, my dear Cottle," he said in excellent English. " I don't mind telling you that I am almost at my last gasp. That fellow Castro has a stranglehold on the country, and I have neither the money nor the men to hold him. Your coming has put new heart into me."

" Well, here I am for what I'm worth, Tenorio," smiled Cottle. " And here's someone who will be much more useful than I. Let me introduce Mr. William Hawkins. There may not be much of him, but he's big enough to handle anything that flies."

The President took Billy's hand in a firm

grasp. " I am delighted to welcome you, Mr. Hawkins. What we' need worse than anything else are airmen. Castro has several planes, though where he got them from I don't know."

" He had a good try at getting ours, sir," said Billy. " But Professor Cottle defeated him. Have you heard how he sunk the rebel launch?"

" I have heard nothing of it," said Tenorio. " Tell me."

So Billy told how Cottle had got the better of the ineffable Garcia, how he had pretended to be meek and mild and ended by leaving the whole gang to swim for their lives.

" Splendid! Splendid!" exclaimed Tenorio in high delight. " But breakfast is waiting. Come, and we will talk where we eat."

The meal was spread in a great cool room, and Billy met all sorts of delicacies which he had not previously encountered, and was young enough to thoroughly enjoy them.

" I want to know all about Castro," said the Professor. " You wrote me that he was buying stuff abroad with this green gold. Have you any idea where he gets it?"

" Yes, but not definitely. All that I can tell you is that somewhere up in the wild mountainous country in the extreme north-west of San Lucar he has found some ancient hoard. The story is that there in the heart of the mountains lies the lost city of Ambala, and it is supposed that he has found it, and is digging among its treasures."

" But if he has all this gold, sir," put in Billy,

" why doesn't he use it to amuse himself and not waste it on buying guns and planes and things?"

" A good question, Mr. Hawkins, and one not easy to answer. But I think that either Castro wants power as well as money, or that there may be difficulties in the way of his securing sufficient gold from Ambala. At any rate, there is no doubt about the fact that he is preparing to plunge the whole of my country into civil war unless I can stop him."

" That's the rub," said Cottle. " How are we to stop him? What are you doing, Tenorio?"

" I have been trying to cut off his supplies, but so far without success."

" How is he getting them in?" asked Cottle. " I thought there was no way except by the railway up to Las Cruces."

" Unfortunately there is. I have discovered that he is getting his munitions up the Orija River. It is only a small stream but large enough to allow launches to pass up. And since it runs into the Amazon I have no control over the mouth of it."

" But the Orija does not run very far up," said Cottle. " Castro must be taking his stuff up into the hills by mule train. Can't you cut his communications?"

" That is exactly what I have been trying to do. I sent a force up under my nephew Almeida, but this is the rainy season and the floods are out. The whole of the forest up in the Luris district is under water, and Almeida cannot cross it."

" What price our plane?" put in Billy.

" Couldn't we buzz up there and bomb Castro's outfit?"

" If you could such help would be simply invaluable," declared the President. " It would, at any rate, delay Castro so as to give me a little more time to organise resistance."

" I'll have a shot at it, sir, if you like," said Billy eagerly. " How far is it?"

" About two hundred miles from here. Is that too far?"

" Not for our bus," replied Billy confidently. " By the by, I suppose there's no petrol to be got up that way?"

" Not beyond Luris, but at Luris itself, which is on the edge of the flooded country, there is plenty. Almeida has lorries with him."

" Top-hole!" exclaimed Billy, and turned to Cottle. " Do you agree, sir?"

" Yes, Billy. And it will be good practice for us. We want to learn something of the country before starting on our big flight."

" Big flight!" repeated Tenorio. " I don't understand."

" Why, to Ambala, of course. The secret city. Surely you want us to get hold of this green gold."

The President's eyes widened. " Madness!" he exclaimed. " The distance is at least six hundred miles. How could you take petrol for the double flight?"

" We can't. We thought we would help ourselves to some of Castro's."

" What! You two alone?"

77

Cottle smiled. " Well, we can't take an army. That's one thing sure. But we don't mind taking a few risks, do we, Billy?"

" Not with you along, sir," replied Billy with his cheery grin.

" It is madness," declared the President again. " Two men against many hundreds. Pray put it out of your mind."

" We'll take our trial trip first, anyhow," said Cottle. " The plane is already unpacked, President. When Billy here has tuned her up we can be off at once. When do you expect the next of Castro's consignments?"

" Almeida has spies who have warned us that another mule train will go up on Thursday next. This is Tuesday. Will you be able to manage that?"

" Like a bird," grinned Billy. " And now, sir, if you will allow me, I will go down to the hangars and get on with my work."

CHAPTER EIGHT

BREAKING BRIDGES

AT dawn on Thursday morning a small party, consisting of Tenorio and some of his officers, watched the big Dolphin take off from the flying-ground just outside Las Cruces. Billy had tried her out on the previous day and her great engine was running like silk as she lifted into the cool air above the forest and sped away to the north. " I always did say there was no way of travelling to touch flying," declared Cottle through the phone. " How's the air, Billy?"

" Fine at present, but it won't be so good when the sun is up."

The sun rose and, as the heat increased, columns of hot air rose, making the Dolphin bump badly. Billy shoved her nose up, and at four thousand feet found better conditions. The country reeled away behind them like a cinema film, and it was not yet half-past seven when Cottle pointed ahead to where a small town stood on a piece of rising ground. " That must be Luris," he said. " The country beyond is all under water."

" Any place to land?" asked Billy.

" No, I can't see anything that looks promising. There's plenty of water, it's true, but there are trees sticking up out of it everywhere. I think we had better push on. The chances are that the convoy will be on the move. They always start in the cool of the morning."

" Right ho!" replied Billy. " Hallo, there's Tenorio's flag."

Sure enough, the blue-and-yellow flag of San Lucar was being hoisted, and men in uniform were staring up at the plane.

" Almeida's crowd," said Cottle as he waved to them.

The plane shot on across the flooded forest. The flooded belt was not wide, but from above it looked a most awkward place to cross, for great belts of tall swamp grass barred the way to boats and it was too deep to wade. Beyond the ground rose a little and in the next valley they could see a thread of water which was no doubt the Orija River.

Billy came lower, at the same time throttling down as much as he dared, and Cottle with his glasses examined the country beyond. " There's the trail," he said presently. " See it, Billy?"

" Yes, but I don't see anything on it. Which way shall I go—west or east?"

" West, I should say. If the convoy left the river at dawn they ought to be some miles to the west by now."

Billy swung the plane and flew westwards. Two minutes had hardly passed before Cottle spoke again. " I've spotted them, Billy. There are about fifty mules all well laden."

" Poor beasts!" said Billy. " I do hate slaying animals, but I suppose there's no help for it."

" And men too," replied Cottle more gravely

than usual. " Tell you what, Billy. Push on a bit and go low."

Billy wondered but obeyed. The plane roared close over the heads of the convoy, and the mules, terrified out of their senses, bolted off the track and away into the forest, scattering their loads in every direction. The Professor chuckled. " That'll give 'em something to think about," he said. " Go ahead, Billy. Keep over the track."

Billy saw that his companion was carefully watching the ground beneath, and a few minutes later he signed to Billy. " Here's what we want. Look down."

Billy looked down. The ground was higher here, and just ahead the path was cut by a deep gorge. The track crossed this by a bridge built in primitive fashion of two great tree trunks laid across the gorge with heavy timber nailed to form the roadway. " I get you," grinned Billy. " This is where we use our bombs."

" Exactly. If we bust up this bridge it will take them at least a week to build a new one, and the chances are that we shall find one or two more farther on."

" All right, sir," said Billy. " I'll take her as low as I dare, and you do the bombing. But we mustn't waste too much time, for the weather is looking a bit dicky."

While he spoke he dropped a little, and as the plane came over the bridge, stalled as much as he dared. The Dolphin, in his capable hands, behaved beautifully, and Cottle, at the very first shot, dropped one of his patent bombs slap on the bridge. It was the same sort of bomb he had used on Garcia's launch, and exploded in a gush of fierce flame which spread at once in a broad patch across the roadway. Billy circled and came back, but there was no need to use a second bomb, for the timbering was already blazing furiously. " Wonderful stuff!" exclaimed Billy.

" It's a little mixture of my own," said Cottle. " Something like thermit, only more so. It'll melt steel, let alone burn timber. Now try for another, Billy."

Billy glanced round. As is usual in the morning during the rainy season in a tropical country, the sky was already clouding up, and down in the south-east, in the direction from which they had come, was turning an ugly blue-black. " I don't awfully care for the look of that," said Billy. " I want to be above it when it does come."

" We've got half an hour, I should think," answered the other.

" That ought to be enough," said Billy as he sent the machine onwards. They flew for about ten miles up the trail before they found a second bridge, and this was so overhung with huge trees that it was most difficult to get at. Three times Billy circled and three bombs were dropped, but each in turn struck among the branches of the forest giants and dropped flaring into the depths of the ravine.

" One more try," said Cottle with set lips, and once more Billy swung the plane, bringing her dangerously close to the tops of the trees. Cottle dropped his fourth bomb. "Hurray!" he shouted. "That's done it." And almost as he spoke such a gust struck them that the Dolphin was flung sideways like a leaf, and only Billy's supreme airmanship saved her from disaster.

"We're for it now," he panted as he turned into the teeth of the gale and started to climb.

"It certainly looks like it," allowed Cottle. "I never thought it would work up so quickly."

Anything more terrifying than the outlook could hardly be imagined. A huge cloud, intensely black and rimmed with rolling white vapour, was rushing up at them with terrific speed. Its dark heart was seamed with streaks and ribands of electric fire, but the thunder was completely drowned by the appalling roar of the wind.

"Can you get above it?" cried Cottle.

"I doubt it," Billy answered with set face, but he opened his throttle to the widest and the plane drove upwards in the teeth of the storm. Up and up she went until the cloud caught and overwhelmed her, shutting off all view of the country beneath. Then came the rain lashing savagely. The darkness became intense but was lit every instant with blazing serpents of blue and white. Thunder cracked deafeningly all around them.

Never had Billy encountered or even imagined anything like this fury of the elements. "Surely we must get above it soon," was his thought, yet though the needle of the barograph registered seven, eight, nine thousand feet in succession the black mist still enveloped them. Billy could only trust to his instruments and carry on. For an hour or more he fought the raging storm, then at last it began to moderate.

Cottle, who in spite of his overcoat shivered with the cold at this great height, heaved a sigh of relief. " The worst is over, Billy."

" I'm not so sure of that," Billy answered gravely.

" What do you mean, Billy?"

" I mean that we've burnt the most fearful lot of petrol in the last hour, and that we shan't have enough to take us back."

" Then we must get some more at Luris," said Cottle. " Tenorio said they had plenty."

" You forget," replied Billy quietly. " You saw, yourself, that there was no place to land anywhere near the town."

Cottle pursed his lips. " You're right. I'd quite forgotten that. Billy, this is going to be awkward."

Billy allowed the Dolphin to drop earthwards in a long volplane, and all the time his quick eyes were searching the country to right and left. " Since we haven't enough spirit to take us back to Las Cruces we must come down somewhere," he said. " And I take it that Luris is the only place where we can be sure of a supply of petrol."

" The only place I know of," Cottle told him.

" Then there's our landing-place," remarked Billy, pointing to an open glade which lay to the north of the road and between the forest and the Orija River.

Cottle frowned. " Right in the enemy's

country, Billy," he said doubtfully. "And— what's worse—on the wrong side of that infernal swamp."

"It's Hobson's choice," said Billy. "There's no other landing-place within miles. The only alternative is to start back for Las Cruces, fly as far as we can and probably crash in the forest. It's practically all trees from here to the capital."

"That's a fact," said Cottle. "Yet if we descend here some of Castro's crowd will be sure to spot us, and even if we get away with our lives, we shall lose the plane."

Billy shook his head. "I don't think so. The clouds are still thick and it's raining hard be-neath us. If I take her down at once and land without using my engine the chances are that no one will be the wiser. And, mind you, the last thing any of the rebels will be expecting is that we should come down so close to them. They saw us going away to the west and they certainly have not spotted us coming back."

"I'll trust you, Billy," said Cottle frankly. "You are boss in a show of this kind."

Billy flushed a little. "I know it's a risk, but I think it's the only thing to be done," he said quietly, and at once set to dropping towards the glade.

Just as he had prophesied, rain was still fall-ing thickly in the lower levels, so thickly indeed that it was by no means easy to see the ground. But Billy's luck was equal to his skill, and after an anxious few moments he brought the big plane safely to earth in the glade.

The glade was about half a mile long, oval in shape and nowhere more than two hundred yards wide. The ground, fairly firm, was covered with coarse grass which, however, had been pretty well grazed down. As the Dolphin came to ground a small knot of cattle galloped away in terror, their tails straight up in the air.

" Cattle mean people," said Cottle gravely. " Yes, and there's a shanty of sorts." He pointed as he spoke to a log-framed building, thatched with reeds, which stood among the trees quite close at hand. His face set hard. " Billy, if any of Castro's people live in that place we're in for trouble."

" Then we'd best take the bull by the horns," replied Billy. " I mean, we'd betted tackle 'em at once, hadn't we?"

" Them's my sentiments," answered the other quietly as he slipped out of his seat and looked at his pistol.

It was still raining while the two walked rapidly across the sopping grass towards the house. As they came nearer they could see a little thin blue smoke coming from the chimney, then suddenly a man stepped out of the door. A tall, thin, brown-faced man with a Winchester rifle in his hands. Before the others were within pistol range he raised his weapon to his shoulder, and, speaking in Spanish, curtly ordered them to halt.

" No choice, Billy," whispered Cottle. " Stand still; I'll do the talking."

The man came slowly forward. His face was hard but not, so Billy thought, a bad one.

86

" Who are you, and what do you want?" he demanded harshly.

" We are English," Cottle replied, " and all we want is shelter from the rain and, if you will be kind enough to give it us, a cup of coffee."

" English?" repeated the other suspiciously. " How came you here?"

At this moment the rain mist thinned and the man caught sight of the plane. His eyes widened. " You are the men with the bird machine," he exclaimed. " It is you who have driven the convoy off the road an hour since?"

Cottle looked hard at him for an instant before replying, and Billy remembered his queer gift of thought reading. His delightful smile crossed Cottle's face. " It would be useless to deny it," he said.

" Then you come from Las Cruces?" stated the man.

" Quite true, my friend. We are of Tenorio's men."

Billy gasped at this bold confession, but evidently Cottle knew what he was about, for instantly the stranger's expression changed, he lowered his rifle and stepped forward. " Por Dios, but I am glad to see you," he said cordially. " But why have you descended here? Surely it is known to you that this is the country of Castro?"

" It was of necessity, not choice. We are out of spirit," said Cottle.

" But there is spirit at Luris. Could you not have gone so far?"

" Quite easily, but at Luris is no open ground large enough to descend."

" I understand," said the other, then looked quickly round. " The rain is ceasing, and any one entering the savanna will see your machine. It would be wise to hide it among the trees."

" That is easy if you will help," said Billy, and to his surprise the man smiled and nodded. " I know little English," he said. " My name Marcos. Once I live in Demerara."

With Marcos' help they rolled the Dolphin in among the trees and Marcos cut green branches to cover her. Then Marcos took them into his little house and gave them hot coffee, and with the food they themselves had brought they made a second breakfast.

" Now what about the petrol, Marcos?" asked Cottle. " Is there any way of getting to Luris and bringing the tins back with us?"

Marcos looked thoughtful. " It will be difficult, señores," he answered. " Between us and Luris lies a bad swamp."

" That I know," replied Cottle. " We saw it from the air and it looked an ugly place."

" It is very bad," agreed Marcos. " Yet not so bad as in the dry season."

Billy opened his eyes. " Not so bad in dry weather?" he repeated. " What does he mean, Professor? Surely the more water the worse it is?"

" Not so," said Marcos. " In the dry season there is still mud to swallow a church, but now
88

there is water to float a boat. You understand, señor?''

'' Of course I do,'' replied Billy. '' I was an idiot not to see it at first. Well then, if we can get a boat we are all right. Is there one to be had, Marcos?''

'' There is one,'' Marcos told him, '' but it is old and leaks.''

'' So long as she will float at all, we'll make do,'' declared Billy. '' What about it? Shall we be shifting?''

A horrified expression crossed Marcos' brown face. '' It is impossible,'' he exclaimed. '' At this time the rebels will be abroad upon the road. We cannot move until the sun has set.''

'' What!'' Billy groaned. '' Got to waste the whole day?''

'' There is shade, there is food and drink,'' replied Marcos. '' Cannot you be content?''

'' I suppose we have to be,'' replied Billy ruefully. '' Anyhow, we are one up on Castro. We've blown two of his bridges to blazes.''

'' It has been a good day's work, señores,'' said Marcos soberly. '' You have earned your rest. Sleep, I beg of you, for I will warn you if danger approaches.''

Billy stretched his arms and yawned. '' I could do with forty winks,'' he observed. '' All right, Señor Marcos; we will be guided by you.''

Marcos showed him a hammock slung under the trees, close to the house, and Billy climbed into it. He was not sorry to get a rest. Also, he had a shrewd suspicion that there was not going to be much sleep for Cottle or himself during the coming night. He dozed off while Marcos and Cottle talked quietly inside the house, but all the time keeping good watch on the open ground outside.

Billy slept solidly for four hours, then roused and made Cottle take his place. The sky had cleared and the sun beat down hotly on the savanna. Once or twice Billy heard sounds of men riding up the trackway on the far side of the meadow, but the trees hid them, and no one came into sight.

" They never come here unless they come after my cattle," Marcos told him. " The dirty thieves, they stole two of my best beasts yesterday. A pest upon the vermin!"

They talked until the shadows began to lengthen, then Marcos set to cooking supper. Marcos was a good cook and his " frijoles," a sort of batter cake, were excellent. While Billy made a capital meal the sun set, and almost at once night settled on the forest.

" It's lucky for us there's a moon," said the Professor. " Even so, it's going to be precious dark under the trees."

He was right. Alone, Billy would never have reached the edge of the swamp, and when they did reach it and had embarked in Marcos' crazy old boat, Billy could hardly believe that they could ever find their way through such a place. Not a ray of moonlight penetrated the huge canopy of branches matted overhead, and the water across which they paddled was like a pool of ink.

Marcos had brought a gun and this he handed to Cottle. " It is loaded with buckshot, señor," he told Cottle, " but do not shoot unless it is necessary."

" Alligators?" suggested Cottle.

" No, señor; what I fear is the anaconda."

" Sort of snake, isn't it?" asked Billy.

" It is the great water python," exclaimed the Professor. " The largest of all snakes. But, Marcos, I did not know that the anaconda attacked man."

" It attacks anything that moves," Marcos told him. He shivered slightly as he spoke, and Billy realised that he was badly scared.

" Do they give any warning?" asked Cottle.

" Their breath is the only warning," said Marcos.

" Their breath?" repeated Billy.

" Yes, it is poison, and paralyses all creatures. Should one attack, at once cover your mouth and nostrils with your handkerchief, for otherwise you will be helpless even to fire a gun."

" Seems a sweet kind of beast," grinned Billy. " Sort of poison-gas machine and tank combined."

" Of a truth he is nothing to laugh about," replied Marcos gravely, as he cleverly avoided the trunk of a huge tree which seemed to bar their way.

" Phew, but these mosquitoes are the limit!" growled Billy presently, as he slapped at

the stinging swarms which plastered his cheeks.
" And what a row those frogs make!"

The noise was simply amazing. Bull frogs
boomed like bitterns, tree frogs bleated like
lambs, all sorts of queer insects up in the towering jungle overhead rattled and whistled and
chuckled in the one deafening chorus. The hot,
thick air was full of the harsh reek of decaying
vegetation, and added to it all was a sensation
of brooding danger which even the light-hearted
Billy did not enjoy.

At last the blackness changed to faint light as
the moon broke through from above and cast
pale gleams upon the black, oily surface of the
water.

" Go slowly," warned Marcos. " Sentries are
posted near the swamp in case of an attack by
rebels. But I have a pass call, and they know
my voice." A little farther on he stopped the
boat altogether, and, pursing up his lips, whistled
three notes. Again and again he whistled, and
at last from somewhere in front came an answering whistle, then a voice demanding to know who
was approaching. Marcos answered, and the
voice ordered them to advance. Next moment
the boat glided out of the swamp tangle into clear
water, and came to rest against a little pier of
rough logs. Two men with rifles stepped forward,
and a third directed the light of an electric torch
upon the boat.

" So it is you, Marcos," said this man in a tone
of relief. " What news have you, and who are
these foreigners that you bring?"

CHAPTER NINE

THE TERROR OF THE SWAMP

EXPLANATIONS were quickly made, and one of
the sentries was detailed to take them up to
Almeida's headquarters while the others guarded
the boat. Almeida was a slight, fair-haired young
man, a complete contrast to his swarthy
followers, and was delighted to see them. '' I
have been worried stiff about you,'' he said in
excellent English. '' We saw you pass over this
morning and we heard you bombing the bridges,
then the storm came and we saw no more of you.
I was terribly afraid that you had crashed in the
forest, and it is the greatest relief to learn that
you are safe. All I regret is the loss of
your machine.''

'' Bless you, she ain't lost,'' said Billy.
'' She's safe as a house over by Marcos' place.
The only trouble is that we are short of petrol.
If you can let us have a dozen cans we shall be
back in Las Cruces for breakfast.''

Almeida shook his head. '' You are welcome
to the spirit, Mr. Hawkins,'' he said gravely,
'' but it will be out of the question to get it back
to the plane. The moon is now high, and we are
expecting an attack from the rebels. My spies
have brought me warning of this, and if you
attempt to return through the swamp you will

certainly be killed. The miracle is that you got across without being seen."

Billy's jaw tightened. "Then you suggest that we leave the Dolphin to the enemy?"

Almeida shrugged. "I trust that they may not discover her, in which case by to-morrow night we may be able to send a party across to destroy her. That is, I fear, all that I can do for you."

"Thanks," said Billy briefly. "All I ask you to do for me is to provide the petrol. Professor Cottle and I will do the rest."

Almeida flushed and Cottle hastened to interfere. "Mr. Hawkins and I are responsible to President Tenorio only," he said quietly, and handed a note from the President himself.

Almeida read it and shrugged his shoulders. "Very good, señor," he said; "this note relieves me of all responsibility, yet I feel it my duty to tell you that any attempt on your part to cross the swamp to-night is equivalent to suicide."

"What time do you expect the attack?"

"Within an hour, though it may not come before midnight."

"Then if we get off at once we have a chance of being back before it comes," replied Cottle. "If you can let us have the petrol we will be off."

"You shall have the petrol," said Almeida, and turned to give instructions to one of his men.

No time was wasted in getting the cans and loading up the boat, and very soon all was ready for the return trip. "Just on eleven," said Cottle, glancing at his watch. "Nothing moving yet. Marcos, is there?"

"Not that I can hear, señor, but the frogs croak so loudly that they drown lesser sounds."

"Come," said Billy who was wild to get back to his beloved Dolphin. "I believe this attack is nothing but a mare's nest. I can't think that Castro's chaps would be fools enough to go boating in the swamp at midnight."

Apparently Billy was right, for they crossed the more open water on the Luris side without seeing or hearing anything of the enemy, and presently entered the denser growth. The moon was now high in the sky, and even in these darksome depths under the enormous canopy of vegetation there was an occasional gleam of light. They were about half-way across when suddenly Marcos stopped paddling and signed to Billy to do the same.

"What's up?" whispered Billy.

"Oars," replied Cottle. "Don't you hear?"

"I do," replied Billy. "Better hide, hadn't we?"

Cottle spoke to Marcos and they pushed the boat into a clump of reeds. They were only just in time, for she was hardly hidden before a punt-shaped craft, long and narrow and packed with men, came silently past.

The three crouched down and kept absolutely still, hardly daring to breathe while the enemy craft passed within a score of yards. It slipped away into the gloom and they waited anxiously to see if any other was coming. But nothing else appeared and presently Marcos signed to proceed. " But be careful," he whispered. " The slightest sound will betray us."

They were hardly clear of the reeds before they ran into another patch of swamp jungle where giant saw grass rose to a height of eight or ten feet above their heads. A narrow lane of stagnant water cut through it and into this Marcos turned the boat. The channel twisted right and left and the tall grass arched over it till it was almost dark. Quite suddenly Billy saw two greenish phosphorescent lights which loomed up about a foot apart and about six feet above the bow of the boat.

" What the mischief?" he began, and just then he heard a hissing sound while an odour reached his nostrils, a stench so horrible that he felt as if he had been poisoned. In an instant he had gone sick and dazed, and sat motionless, gazing with fascinated horror at the twin lamps.

" Anaconda!" he heard Marcos gasp out, but even then he could not move.

A hand fell on his shoulder and dragged him down and on the instant a gun roared.

" Back! back!" shouted Marcos as he dug his paddle desperately into the water.

Ahead, pandemonium broke loose. It was as though a huge chain cable had been endowed with life and then gone mad. The tall weeds were mowed down as by giant flails, black water rose in spray, lashed by the awful coils of the dying monster, and broke over the boat. But for Marcos they must have been swamped.

Luckily, the boat was still close to the mouth of the black canal, and Marcos got them out in time. The crashing died away, and the only signs of what had happened were the heavy ripples lapping outwards from the scene of the monster's death agony.

Billy struggled up. "I'm awfully sorry. I got a whiff before I knew what was up. Marcos was right; it fairly paralysed me."

"Don't apologise. I should have been done but for Marcos," replied Cottle. "As it was, I only just managed to pull the trigger."

"You did the trick all right," replied Billy— "blew the brute's head off, I fancy."

"Do not waste time talking," said Marcos in a hissing whisper. "That shot will have been heard for miles. Ah, I thought as much. The rebels' boat has turned and is coming back."

"You are right," said Cottle quietly. "What do we do now—hide?"

"It is our only chance, and that but a slight one," whispered back Marcos. "With only two paddlers and our heavy load, we cannot hope to get clear."

"Where do we hide—in the edge of the grass?" asked Billy.

"No—farther on," replied Marcos. He started to paddle, then stopped. "We can go no farther," he said quickly. "They are too close. They will hear us. Push in here."

They forced the boat into the edge of the grass,

pulled the tall stuff over her and covered her as best they could. Before they had finished, the splash of oars sounded close at hand, and a harsh voice said in Spanish: "This is the spot from which the shot came. Turn on the light, Ricardo."

The glow of an electric torch flashed out across the gloomy water, and Billy shrank down as the bright beam cut through the darkness. His right hand went to the butt of his pistol, for he fully believed that they must be discovered, and that the only thing left was to sell their lives as dearly as possible. Cottle seemed of the same opinion for he had poked the muzzle of his gun over the stern of the boat and lay flat, with his finger on the trigger.

The same voice came again: "There is the passage. There is the way by which they went. Paddle, you dogs! Paddle!"

The big boat shot into the narrow passage from which the three had only just emerged. It was so close to the fugitives that Billy could actually hear the heavy breathing of the men as they dipped their paddles. They were hardly a boat's length away, and if the light were turned in the direction of Marcos's boat the rebels could not help but see it. But they were using the torch to find their way through the channel, and Billy breathed more freely as they passed.

"That's better," he whispered in Cottle's ear.

"I wish I could think so," replied Cottle in an equally low tone. "But they'll find the dead snake and turn back. We're not out of the wood yet, Billy.

" Ah, I told you so," as a sudden shout came out of the rushes.

" Anaconda! Beware! It is the great snake!"

" It's dead, you fool," snapped the leader. " That's what they shot at. But they didn't pass. I'll swear they didn't try to pass while that thing was dying."

" Dios! but see the size of it," cried another; " it's body is like a tree trunk."

" Never mind the size of it," snapped the first speaker. " Back out of this, and quick about it. Those gringos are hiding somewhere in the grass, and we must have them. They are the same for whom Pecos is offering five thousand dollars a head."

" Pecos!" whispered Billy ruefully. " So he's alive! I'd hoped that we had finished with that gentleman. I say, Professor, hadn't we better skip out?"

" It's that or fight," answered Cottle. " They are bound to find us. What do we do, Marcos?"

" We go," whispered Marcos between set teeth, " but "—he added in a tone of deadly certainty—" they will catch us."

" They'll catch a bit of lead as well," Billy promised grimly. " Shove out."

Paddle in hand he stood up and was trying to force the boat out of the tangle of grass when a shot rang out so close that he could see the flash.

Someone shouted wildly, then followed another shot and a third.

" They've spotted us," cried Billy, but his voice was drowned by such a screaming as made his very skin crawl.

" What's up?" he gasped, but Marcos, too, was on his feet. " Push off! Push off!" he cried in terror. " Let us get out of this, for we shall not escape a second time."

For the life of him Billy could not imagine what was up but, in any case, the din within the reeds was so terrible that his one idea was to get as far as possible from it. He paddled furiously and so did Marcos, and it was not until they had reached the landing-place that they stopped.

" What was it?" demanded Billy.

" The snake's mate," Marcos answered.

It was Cottle who explained. " Many snakes hunt in couples," he explained. " I have heard that the water pythons do so, and that when one is killed the other attacks. That's what happened and that's what has saved us."

Billy shivered. " Thanks be that we got out in time," he said as he climbed out of the boat on to dry land, and began to unload the petrol tins.

" Two dozen of them—how are we going to get them across?" asked Cottle.

" I will fetch my bullock cart," said Marcos.

" Good man!" said Cottle. " One of us will stay and guard the tins, the other will help you."

" You stay, sir," said Billy. " I'll go and help harness up."

The Professor agreed, and Billy and Marcos set off. They went cautiously, but all seemed quiet, and to Billy's great relief the plane stood safely where they had left it. They went on to the house, then as they reached it Billy suddenly whipped out his pistol. "Look out, Marcos," he said. "There's a man on the porch."

The man, who was seated on the rough planking by the door with a black cigar between his lips, rose to his feet. "It is I, Benoliel," he said in Spanish.

Marcos relaxed. "A friend, Señor Hawkins. He is a pedlar and well known to me."

"What is he doing here?" inquired Billy. Benoliel stepped out into the moonlight. He was short, stocky, very powerfully built, with a face as swarthy as that of a gipsy. He had a great hooked nose and very dark eyes.

"I greet you, Marcos," he said in a deep bass voice. "But who is this?"

"He is English; a friend of our good President."

"Then I am happy to meet him," said Benoliel. "Without doubt he is one of those who has broken the rebel communications this morning. It is a heavy blow to the scoundrel Castro."

"What are you doing here?" asked Marcos. "This is no safe place for a friend of Tenorio."

"I know it, yet the pedlar trades safely with both friend and foe. I have but now come from the rebel camp, and have spoken with Sid Larkin within the hour."

" Larkin?" repeated Marcos.

" Yes, the Americano who is Castro's friend. I have much information for the President could I but reach him."

" You can reach him all right," said Billy. " I can take you."

Benoliel's dark eyes gleamed. " Excellent!" he exclaimed; " but how?"

Marcos explained, and told him about the petrol.

" The sooner you start the better," advised Benoliel. " For the present the coast is clear, but soon the rebels will be back. Can you give me food? I have not eaten since breakfast."

" Señor Hawkins will find food for you. Myself, I must hasten to harness the cart."

Billy went into the house with Benoliel. " Here is food," he said in his rather halting Spanish, and pointed to the cupboard. " I do not think that there is any fire left in the hearth, but we will light it again and boil some coffee."

" I thank you, señor," said Benoliel. " I will light the fire if you will kindly take the dishes out of the cupboard."

Billy stepped to the cupboard which was in one corner of the room, and in so doing turned his back to the pedlar. Next instant it seemed to him as if the roof had fallen on his head. He crashed to the floor and lay still, completely stunned.

Benoliel stood over him grasping the sandbag with which he had struck the treacherous blow. " Number one," he said with a cruel smile on his thin lips. "That ten thousand dollars will be easily won, and I shall have the aeroplane as well. Now to make him safe," and so saying he set to tying and gagging Billy.

CHAPTER TEN

CAUGHT NAPPING

THE pedlar swiftly finished his job, and, after making sure that Billy could neither move nor speak, went to the door, where he stood motionless, listening. "Ah, Marcos has the oxen harnessed," he said to himself. "Now to settle him."

He gripped his sandbag more firmly and took a step forward. Then he checked. "No," he went on; "that will not do. I must not tackle Marcos yet, for I have the other gringo to settle, and if I go alone he may be suspicious." He stood still for a moment or two, thinking hard. "I have it," he said presently. "I will go with Marcos to fetch these cans of essence for the aeroplane. Then, when safe back among the trees, I can strike down Marcos. Afterwards, I will call to the other that robbers have attacked his friend, and as he enters this door I shall have my chance to stun him."

An ugly grin twisted his thin lips, and hiding the sandbag under his coat he went out to the stall where Marcos had just finished putting the harness on two bullocks. He was busy with the wheels of the cart, and looked up as Benoliel approached. " I am greasing them," he said, " so that they shall not squeak during our journey."

" That is well," said Benoliel. " And now, since I have eaten, I will come with you. The Señor Hawkins will be waiting at the spot where the aeroplane lies. He says that he will have the tank ready to fill when the essence arrives."

" Then let us go at once," said the unsuspecting Marcos. He prodded his oxen with an old-fashioned goad, and they set off at once at a brisk walk, and presently they came safely to where Cottle, seated on a great log, was still keeping guard over the petrol tins.

But when he saw a stranger with Marcos he was on his feet in a moment. " Who is this?" he asked curtly.

" A friend, Señor Professor," replied Marcos, and introduced Benoliel in due form. " He is a pedlar," he explained, " and so travels safely in these dangerous parts."

" That is true, señor," said Benoliel with a greasy smile. " As I have just been telling the Señor Hawkins, I have been in the camp of the enemy to-day, and have even spoken to the Americano, Sid Larkin, who is in command."

" In fact you have been doing a little spy work?" suggested Cottle in his excellent Spanish.

Benoliel shrugged his shoulders. " It is not nice work, I will admit, señor. Yet it is necessary, and if I can help to crush this revolution

I shall feel myself well repaid for any danger I have incurred. El Señor Tenorio has been kind to me, and I have for him a great admiration."

" We all have that," said Cottle. " Then I take it you will wish to accompany us to the capital to-morrow?"

" That is so, señor. The Señor Hawkins has promised to take me, for, without boasting, I can say that I have much valuable information for the President's private ear."

" That is good," said Cottle heartily. " Then let us be moving."

Marcos loaded up the tins of petrol, and they started back. Cottle walked close alongside Benoliel, chatting with him all the way. The pedlar tried to answer easily, but he had never met any one in the least like Cottle, and for the life of him he could not size him up. They reached the spot where the plane stood under the trees and Benoliel expressed surprise that Billy was not there. " He said he would have all ready to fill the tank," he explained to Cottle.

" He is waiting for us in the house, I have no doubt," said Cottle. " Heating some coffee, I expect. Help me to unload the petrol, Señor Benoliel, then Marcos can put his oxen away in their stall."

Benoliel hesitated, for this did not chime with his plans. But only for an instant. Left alone with Cottle, he could wait his chance and strike him down, and after that Marcos would be easy prey. He set to unloading the cans. This took but a few moments, then Marcos drove away through the trees towards the house, leaving Cottle alone with the pedlar.

" We may as well put the petrol straight into the tank," said Cottle quietly. " I will open the tank if you will be good enough to unscrew the tops of the tins."

He turned his back on Benoliel and walked towards the plane. In a flash Benoliel had slipped his horrible weapon loose from its hiding-place under his coat, and leaped after the other. Then, exactly as though he had eyes in the back of his head, Cottle ducked to one side, and the sand-bag, instead of striking him on the skull, thudded harmlessly against the ground. The force of the blow threw Benoliel off his balance, and, before he could recover it, Cottle had sprung upon him from behind. The pedlar went sprawling on his face, and Cottle's weight knocked the breath from his body, leaving him gasping in silent agony.

" You poor fish!" said Cottle as he wrenched the sandbag from his enemy's nerveless fingers. Then he pulled both the man's arms round behind his back, and with his handkerchief fastened his wrists tightly together. Rising leisurely, he jerked Benoliel to his feet. " Get to the house, you swine," he ordered, " and if I find that you have hurt Billy, Heaven pity you!"

Breathless and dizzy, the wretched Benoliel had no strength or energy to resist, and Cottle drove him before him to the house. Pushing him in through the door, he held him and looked round. " Billy!" he called. " Billy, where are you?"

There was no answer. Just then the smouldering sticks fell together on the hearth, and a little blaze shot up, by the light of which Cottle saw Billy lying tied and gagged on the floor.

His blue eyes blazed. " You'll be sorry for this," he said to Benoliel, and the tone of his voice made that worthy quiver with such terror as he had never known. Next moment Cottle had tripped him, flinging him down on the floor with a force that almost stunned him. " Move an eyebrow," said Cottle, " and I'll burn you alive." Then he strode across to Billy and, snatching a knife from the table as he passed, rapidly cut him loose. " Are you hurt, my dear boy?" he asked anxiously.

" I've a bit of a headache," Billy answered hoarsely, " but I don't think there's any serious damage done. My word, I am glad to see you, Professor. I've been suffering agonies to think that this swine was after you, and that I couldn't warn you."

" I have my own little warnings," replied Cottle as he picked Billy up and set him in a chair. " I can assure you it did not take me long to size up this beauty. He got the shock of his misspent life when he tried to brain me and found I wasn't there."

Billy chuckled feebly. " I'll bet he did. But tie him up, sir. He's bad medicine."

" I will," said Cottle, and, using the rope with

which Billy had been tied, secured Benoliel's ankles and left him helpless.

At that moment Marcos came in and, seeing Benoliel trussed up, stood staring in amazement. Cottle wasted no time in putting him wise, and poor Marcos was dreadfully upset. " You might think that I too was in the plot, señor, but I assure you I had no suspicion of this man," he protested.

" Do not trouble your head, my friend," said Cottle quietly. " As it happens, I am something of a thought reader, and I was as certain of your innocence as of his guilt. He tried to brain me, and if he had succeeded you would have been his next victim. You see, there is a price on our heads, and he meant to have it."

" The dog!" snorted Marcos. " What shall we do with him, señor—hang him?"

" He deserves it," said Cottle, and the wretched spy shivered. " But I don't feel disposed to turn executioner. We must think of some other method of disposing of him."

" We might take him with us to Las Cruces," suggested Marcos.

" Yes, but there will be no room in the plane. At most we can only carry three, and I believe you wish to go with us, Marcos?"

" Certainly it will not be safe for me to remain here, señor," said the man.

A faint chuckle came from the chair where Billy was lying. " I know what we can do with him, Professor," said Billy.

Cottle and Marcos both turned to Billy.

"We'll hand him over to Almeida," said Billy.

"What—cross that swamp again? Nothing doing, Billy," replied Cottle.

"Not in the boat," said Billy. "In the plane."

Cottle looked puzzled. "You're a bit muzzy, Billy, I'm afraid. No wonder, after that crack on the head. You've forgotten there is no landing-place."

"Forgotten nothing," Billy answered. "We don't have to descend. There's a parachute aboard. We'll drop him."

A howl of terror came from the wretched Benoliel. "I knew he'd like the notion," grinned Billy. "But it will work quite nicely. You'll come up with me, Professor, and put him over. Then we'll come back for Marcos. What do you think of my plan, Marcos?"

"I would throw him over, but not with a parachute," returned Marcos grimly.

Cottle spoke. "Your idea is a good one, Billy," he said, "but the one objection is that it means keeping the fellow here for some days until you are able to fly."

"Some days!" repeated Billy. "What are you talking about, sir? You and I are going to breakfast with the President to-morrow—I mean this morning. There's nothing the matter with me except a headache, and a cup of coffee will put that to rights."

Cottle looked hard at him. "You are a bit of a wonder, Billy," he remarked. "You shall have your coffee, then, if you are really fit to fly, the sooner we leave the better."

Billy had his coffee, and the way in which he revived amazed Cottle. Within half an hour he vowed that he was fit to start. But this the Professor would not allow.

"We will go at dawn," he said. "Meantime, you must get a couple of hours' sleep, Billy."

Billy grinned, rolled on to a cot, and within five minutes was sound off.

The grey was turning to pink as the Dolphin's big engine burst into life, sending echoes rattling through the sleeping forest. "Pity someone doesn't invent a silent engine," remarked Billy as he took his seat. "We're advertising ourselves a bit more than I like. Is all ready, Professor?"

"Yes. I'm in my seat, and the Benoliel beast is safely stowed aft. Let her rip, Billy."

The crack on his head did not seem to have affected Billy to any serious extent, for the Dolphin lifted sweetly and surely and within a few moments was soaring high above the swamp. On the far side Luris lay among its trees.

"I wonder how Almeida fared last night," said Billy. "I shouldn't fancy he had much trouble in whacking that gang of rebels. But here we are. Are you ready to drop the pedlar person?"

"Quite ready," replied Cottle coolly. "The parachute is fixed to him, and I have a note ready to drop to tell Almeida what to do with him."

"Right you are. Then shove him over."

Benoliel was limp with terror, and Cottle had

to prod him with the muzzle of his pistol to force him over the edge of the body. " If you don't hurry you'll go without the parachute," he threatened. Over with you! "

Billy heard a shriek and felt the plane lurch. He banked, and caught a glimpse of their prisoner's body shooting downwards. Then the big parachute began to balloon outwards, checking the speed of the fall, and in another few seconds was dropping as lightly as a soap bubble with Benoliel swinging pendulum fashion at the end of his rope.

" Bit of a surprise for Almeida! " grinned Billy. " Ah, they've heard us at last. Watch 'em! They're coming out like bees swarming. I'll drop a little so that you can chuck over your message." He shut off and had started to plane downwards when Cottle's voice cut the sudden silence. " Up with you! Up, Billy! Quickly, or it will be too late."

Instead of asking the reason, Billy instantly obeyed, but the big machine had hardly begun to rise before a number of little bursts of smoke appeared among the trees below and bullets came screaming past. Two, at least, struck the body of the plane, but did no serious harm. Billy gave her all she would take, and she swept off at terrific speed until they were a couple of miles away and at the five-thousand-foot level. Then he turned to Cottle. " Has Almeida gone mad or have we? " he questioned.

" Neither," Cottle answered curtly. " The rebels have taken Luris."

Billy gasped. " Jumping Jupiter, but that's just what must have happened! I say, this is a bad job for Almeida."

" And for Tenorio—and ourselves," replied Cottle. " Billy, we have to pick up Marcos. You had better not waste time about it, for we shall have the whole hornets' nest about our ears. You can take it that they are all wised up to what has happened."

" If they are not, Benoliel will tell them," growled Billy.

It was only a matter of a couple of minutes before the Dolphin had dropped again into the savanna. Marcos, who had been watching, came across towards her with a bundle on his back. " Hurry!" shouted Billy, making a trumpet of his hands, and Marcos broke into a run. Next moment there came the sharp bark of a field-gun, and a shell soared across the swamp and fell about fifty yards beyond the plane, bursting with a roar and flinging up a great fountain of earth.

" That's torn it!" growled Billy.

" I thought as much," said Cottle. " They have sized up our plans pretty neatly, or more likely the pedlar fellow has got down safely and told them. Shift her a bit, Billy."

Billy started the engine again and taxied in an easterly direction. It was lucky that he did so, for next moment a second shell pitched almost on the very spot where the plane had been standing."

" How in thunder have they got the range?"

demanded Billy. " Surely they haven't a plane of their own?"

" Not a plane," said Cottle, " but look there!" He pointed as he spoke in the direction of the river, and high above the trees a big, ugly-looking sausage balloon was outlined against the blue. Billy whistled softly. " I hadn't reckoned on that, Professor. Castro's more up to date than I'd thought."

" You can take it he's been using that green gold of his to good purpose," replied Cottle. " But keep her shifting, Billy. It's our only chance."

" How the mischief are we to pick up Marcos then?" groaned Billy, and the words were hardly out of his mouth before a third shell came howling from Luris. It struck the ground between the plane and Marcos, and when the smoke cleared there was poor Marcos flat on the ground.

" The brutes! They've got him," groaned Billy.

" I'll get him," said Cottle sharply, and as Billy stopped the machine Cottle leapt out and ran with long strides towards the prostrate man. Before he reached him two shells fell almost simultaneously, one so near that the plane rocked with the concussion and bits of earth stung Billy's cheek.

Now for the first time Billy felt really scared. With two guns at work it looked as if the plane must be hit, and if it was smashed or even damaged it was all up with the three of them.

And not only that, but probably with Tenorio also.

Cottle had reached Marcos and hoisted the man on his back. But he had a good two hundred yards to carry him, and with such a weight could move but slowly. Crash! came another shell, this, luckily, a bit short, yet well on the line.

Suddenly Billy's eyes fell upon the row of neat little bombs ranged in a rack beside him, and he remembered that they were not all explosive but some were smoke bombs. Quick as thought he had two of them out of the casing and had flung them out on to the ground. They burst at once and up rolled a huge cloud of heavy, black, greasy smoke.

Inside ten seconds the smoke fog lay like a solid wall between him and the observers, and Billy ventured to turn a little in the direction where Cottle was struggling along with Marcos. " Good man! " panted the Professor as he came alongside. " Help me in with him."

" Is he dead? " asked Billy anxiously as they heaved Marcos into the body of the plane.

" No, thanks be. Only stunned," answered Cottle as he scrambled in. " And now get out of it as quickly as you can, Billy. This is a bit too hot to suit me."

CHAPTER ELEVEN

ANOTHER SURPRISE PACKET

As the Dolphin rose, two shells smashed into the smoke cloud. " They're making uncommon good practice," remarked Billy.

" Yes, no doubt Castro has got some European gunners——" He stopped abruptly. " Where are you going, Billy? This isn't the way to Las Cruces."

Billy gave him a quick glance. " You didn't want us to sneak off with our tails between our legs, sir?" he exclaimed. " Surely we can get a bit of our own back!"

Cottle smiled crookedly. " You're a blood-thirsty beggar, Billy, but, after all, I suppose you are right. You mean that we should bomb Luris?"

" Why, of course," replied Billy. " We ought not to leave it in the hands of the enemy, and a few of your particular patents will see to that. The place is all wood, and should burn like tinder."

" Yes, but what about the plane, Billy? You must remember this is the only one we've got. It gives me cold chills to think of anything happening to her."

" Me, too," agreed Billy, " but she'll be a darned sight safer over Luris than on the

savanna. Field-pieces can't be elevated beyond
a certain angle."

Cottle shrugged. " It's your show, Billy. You
know more about these matters than I do. But
here we are. Shall I start in?"

The Dolphin was now right over Luris, and
clearly a very unpleasant surprise for the rebels,
who must have thought that she was smashed up.
Cottle and Billy could see them far below running about like ants. They were firing, too, with
rifles, for bullets came hissing up.

Cottle began dropping bombs. First he put
out a couple of smoke bombs just to get the
range, and these, falling right among the houses,
burst into jetty balls of impenetrable smoke.
Then he sent over the fire bombs, and the second
dropped smack on the roof of a long, shed-like
building.

" That's done it!" cried Billy. " Jumping
Jupiter, look at her burn!"

Indeed, it seemed impossible that so tiny
a missile could produce such an effect, for within
a few seconds a sheet of flame rose from the
doomed building and a column of smoke came
straight up into the windless air. Within five
minutes the whole place was alight, and the
rebels, seeing it was hopeless to save the town,
were bolting away down a road leading through
the forest.

Billy chuckled grimly. " That's that," he
said. " Luris won't be much use to Larkin and
Co. I only hope Almeida has got away."

Cottle pointed to a little village some miles to

the south. " He and his men are over there," he said. " I can see Tenorio's flag above one of the houses. And now, Billy, we'd best be shifting if, as you promised, we are to breakfast with the President."

Billy looked round and pointed to the sausage which hung defiantly above the forest near the river. " We can't leave them that, sir. With your permission, we will put just one bomb on top of it before we go home."

" You're crazy, Billy. They have guns there, remember!"

" I know. They have been blazing away at us for the last five minutes," grinned Billy.

" Shooting at us?"

" Yes. There goes another shell," replied Billy, pointing to a dark puff against the blue. " But I don't wonder you were none the wiser, for not one has burst within a quarter of a mile. Honestly, Professor, there's no risk to speak of."

" Oh, go ahead," said Cottle with a resigned air, and Billy sent the Dolphin roaring back once more across the swamp.

" That's rattled them," he chuckled as two field-pieces spoke at once, but with such hopeless aim that the shells burst many hundreds of yards behind and below the Dolphin. Before the rebels could fire again, Billy was above them, and he and Cottle were amazed to see what a collection of buildings lay behind the wharf which bordered the river. But for the moment all Billy's attention was centred upon the balloon. The observers had seen the plane coming and both had jumped.

Of course, they had parachutes, and seemingly both reached the ground in safety.

"One bomb, sir," said Billy. "And if you miss better use the machine-gun. But first I'll take you right over."

A spiteful crackle of machine-gun fire broke out from below, but Billy paid no attention. He swept close above the sausage, and Cottle neatly dropped one of his deadly little bombs on top of it. Swiftly as Billy passed they could feel the heat from the blast of blazing gas.

"We may as well do in the buildings, sir," said Billy as they shot past and came over the clump of warehouses.

"Look out!" roared Cottle suddenly. The warning came too late. In the hollow square formed by the buildings the black muzzle of a real anti-aircraft gun pointed skywards, and as the Dolphin passed over it only a few hundred feet up, fire burst from it.

Billy felt the Dolphin jerk and quiver, then she was sliding earthwards.

How Billy got down without a crash he never knew. The Dolphin missed the roof of the nearest shed by a matter of feet only, and slid safely to earth at the west end of the hollow square formed by the buildings. She was hardly on the ground before rifles began to crack and bullets came whizzing past.

But Cottle was already at work, and as two of his smoke bombs burst between the plane and the anti-aircraft gun up rushed a mass of black smoke forming an impenetrable curtain between the crew of the Dolphin and their enemies. At the same instant Billy grabbed one of the Madsen machine-guns which Cottle had taken from Pecos' cases, and, scuttling away to one side, flung himself down and opened fire.

A rain of bullets crackled and thudded against the stand of the anti-aircraft gun and tore through the opposite buildings, and at once the rifle fire ceased.

Absolute silence reigned. Billy picked up his gun and crept back towards the Dolphin. "What's up, Professor?" he asked uneasily. " I can't hear a thing. Where are the beggars?"

" Dead, Billy," answered Cottle quietly.

" Dead!" repeated Billy in amazement. " But I was only firing at the anti-aircraft outfit. Where are the rest?"

" There are no rest. Don't you understand? Larkin took his whole force across the swamp last night against Luris, and left no one here except a guard on the gun. You've finished 'em, and the place is ours."

" I'm hanged if I don't believe you are right," said Billy slowly. " But the others will be back. Since we've burnt them out of Luris they are bound to come back."

" All the same, it gives us time to clear," said Cottle. " I suppose we shall have to hoof it back to Las Cruces, and it's a shocking job being forced to abandon the Dolphin. We must, of course, destroy her before we leave."

Billy did not answer at once for he was busy examining the plane. Cottle watched him keenly.

" Billy," he said, " is there any chance of saving her?"

" I—I almost think so," Billy answered in a voice that was not quite so steady as usual. " It is only the tail that is damaged. I believe I can repair it, indeed I am sure I could if I only had the time."

" How long will it take?" demanded Cottle.

" I can't say. But if you can help me, we might manage it in a couple of hours."

Cottle's strong jaw set. " Then we'll have a darned good try at it," he declared. " Get to it, Billy, and tell me what to do." But Billy was already spreading out tools, and next minute set to work with savage energy.

Half an hour passed like five minutes, then Cottle straightened his back and swept the streaming perspiration from his forehead.

" Billy, we don't know when they'll come," he said. " One of us ought to have a look-see."

" I will watch," came a voice, and to the astonishment of them both here was Marcos clambering out of the plane. In their desperate haste they had almost forgotten the poor fellow.

" Can you walk?" asked Cottle as he sprang across to give the man a hand.

" Well enough, señor," Marcos answered. " And my eyes are still good, praise the saints. I promise good warning when those sons of dogs approach."

Cottle glanced after him. " Plenty of pluck the fellow's got. Now, where's that pair of wire nippers, Billy?"

The two set to it again, working with furious energy, and Billy found that the Professor was almost as good a mechanic as himself. At last Billy looked up. " I believe she'll do, sir," he said. And just then Marcos came scuttling round the corner. " They are in sight, señores," he cried. " I see men coming through the trees up from the swamp."

Billy glanced round. " No room to rise here," he said briefly. " We must wheel her out." Luckily there was an opening large enough to allow the plane to get through, but the moment they got outside they heard shouts, and an instant later rifles began to crack. Cottle was ready, and two more of his smoke bombs flung down behind the plane threw up a smoke screen which hid them completely from the enemy. Billy flung himself into his seat and Marcos scrambled in behind. But Cottle had vanished. " Where is he?" demanded Billy. " Where's the Professor?"

" I know not, señor. He was here a moment since, then I lost sight of him in the smoke."

" If he doesn't come soon we are done for," said Billy in despair, for bullets were beginning to rain through the smoke cloud. " If one of those bits of lead happens to hit our tank it's all U P with the lot of us."

" All right, Billy," came Cottle's voice, and, active as a boy, he leaped into his seat. " Let her rip!" he cried.

Billy let her rip. There was a moment of tense anxiety, then the big plane lifted safely, and once she was in the air her pilot breathed a sigh of deepest relief.

Having got his height, Billy swung the Dolphin and turned right back over the buildings where they had spent the last strenuous hour. He began to drop again. " What are you after, my son?" demanded Cottle.

" We have some bombs still," said Billy. " Surely you're not going to leave the beggars all those buildings?"

" We are not going to take any second chances with that long gun," replied Cottle firmly. " Keep her up, Billy, and don't you dare drop an inch."

Billy looked bitterly disappointed. " You're in command, sir," he said coldly.

Cottle laughed outright. " What a blood-thirsty beggar you are, Billy. And, in any case, we are late for breakfast and shall be in luck if we get back in time to lunch with the President."

Billy made no answer. Again Cottle laughed. " Look down, you juggins! Look down!" he said. Billy looked, and beheld a vast cloud of smoke pouring upwards from the rebel store-houses, and beneath them licked out crimson tongues of flame. " My sacred Sam!" gasped Billy. " The show's burning like a bonfire."

" Of course it is," said Cottle. " What do you think I was doing while you were fussing behind the smoke screen?" Billy lifted one hand to the salute. " I apologise, sir. When we get home I'll ask you to kick me."

" Let Larkin do the kicking," smiled the

Professor. "Luris has gone up, and now his own camp is burning. If he isn't kicking himself, he ought to be. Now give her gas, and see if you can't break the speed limit. It's twenty-four hours since I had a bath or a square meal, and I think we have earned both those luxuries."

CHAPTER TWELVE

A DAY'S DELAY

"Some lunch!" said Billy as he laid down his fork and spoon.

"I won't have you talking American," retorted Cottle.

"Then shall I say this has been a real elegant meal?" grinned Billy.

The President laughed. "In any case, you have earned the best I can give you, Mr. Hawkins."

Billy reddened. "You make me feel ashamed, sir. Why, we haven't started yet. Not on the real job of work, anyhow."

"You have put a very big spoke in Castro's wheel," said the President. "It will be weeks before he or that scoundrel Larkin are able to get any more stores up-country."

"I am afraid the damage is done already, President," said Cottle. "From what Marcos tells me, an immense amount of material has gone through. And I think it quite likely that this little business will drive Castro to work sooner than he had otherwise intended."

" That is quite likely," agreed the President. " Unfortunately, I can get very little information as to what is going on beyond Tobosa."

" That's our job, sir," said Billy. " I thought we would overhaul the bus to-day and slip along again to-morrow."

The President stared. " I thought the plane was injured."

" There's not much the matter, sir," said Billy cheerily. " I think we ought to get the job through by night."

" But you and the Professor want rest."

" We'll get a good calk to-night," Billy told him. " And now, if you will excuse me, I'll toddle off to the flying-ground."

" His energy is amazing," said the President to Cottle as Billy hurried off. " Do you think, Professor, the boy quite realises what is before him—and you?"

" I don't suppose he has given it a second thought," replied Cottle. " Billy Hawkins is a fighter, and it was the biggest streak of luck that ever came my way when he walked into my place that evening after he had settled with friend Pecos."

" And for me too," added the President. " Cottle, if I am still President of San Lucar when this business is finished, I'll give that boy complete charge of our new air force and an absolutely free hand."

Cottle laughed. " Time to talk of that when

we've licked Castro. Now I'm going down to the aerodrome."

A car whisked Cottle out to the flying-ground, and there was Billy in overalls, grease to the eyes, working with the mechanics. "She'll be right as rain before dark," he announced. "We can get off good and early to-morrow. Will you see about the grub and stores, Professor?"

"Right, Billy. I will do it at once," replied the other, and went off on his mission. As Billy had promised, all was ready by nightfall, and Marcos, who had been resting all the afternoon, promised to remain in charge during the night. So Billy and the Professor went comfortably off to bed.

Dawn was hardly breaking when Billy was again at the aerodrome. He had already breakfasted and had hurried ahead to get the Dolphin out of her hangar. To his surprise, the door of the hangar, though closed, was unlocked. "Marcos!" he shouted as he hurried in. "Marcos, where are you?"

There was no answer, and Billy, feeling suddenly nervous, switched on the lights. To his horror, there was Marcos lying flat on the floor, apparently either dead or insensible. Billy glanced at the plane, but that, so far as he could see, was uninjured. He flung himself down on his knees beside Marcos to find that the man was breathing and apparently asleep. Then an odd, sweetish smell rose to his nostrils. "Holy smoke!" he gasped, "they've drugged him."

At that moment Cottle came in. "Drugged,"

he repeated. "Who is drugged?" Then he saw Marcos, and, springing forward, set to examining him. "You are right, Billy. The man is drugged. Get me some cold water."

Billy fetched the water, and Cottle, who among his other accomplishments was a doctor of medicine, set to work on Marcos. In a few moments the man was sitting up and staring at the others in a dazed fashion.

"Dios, but I have slept at my post!" he cried.

"You can't help that," replied Cottle. "You have been drugged, man. What have you taken?"

"Nothing but the coffee which I brought with me to keep me awake."

"Someone managed to dope it," Cottle told him. "It's all right, Marcos. We do not blame you." He turned to Billy. "Whoever it is must have been meddling with the plane. Don't let any mechanics in. You and I must go over her to see what's been done to her."

"We shall find the wires cut, or a hole in the tank," said Billy bitterly.

"I doubt it," replied Cottle. "These people go a bit deeper than that, I fancy."

Billy set to work at once and Cottle helped, but the result of the search proved that the Professor was right, for to the Dolphin herself no injury whatever had been done.

"I thought as much," said Cottle gravely. "It's the stuff aboard that has been handled. Either dud bombs have been substituted, or the food has been tampered with. We shall have to get every single thing out of her."

"Then it's all up with starting to-day," growled Billy.

"Better twenty-four hours' delay than taking foolish chances," was the answer. "Billy, you don't yet realise what we are up against, and," he added to himself, "I'm not so sure that I do, either."

Cottle and Billy did the work with their own hands. Every bomb was taken out and replaced, also every scrap of food and drink; the tank, too, they emptied and filled with fresh petrol, while every drop of oil was drained out and changed.

That night Billy and Cottle themselves spent on guard in the hangar, relieving one another every three hours.

At six next morning all was ready and the President himself came down to see them off. Before they started he called them aside. "This is to be a scouting excursion only," he said firmly. "I want you both to promise me that you will not attempt to descend at or near Tobosa. You do promise this, Professor?"

"Yes, President, I will give you my word on that," replied Cottle quietly.

"And you too, Mr. Hawkins," continued Tenorio. "Will you give me your word?"

"I suppose I've got to," said Billy reluctantly. "Still, if they start shooting at us, I suppose you won't mind our dropping a bomb or two."

" I would rather you did not even do that. What I require is news of Castro's forces and stores. That will be of the greatest possible value to me. Later, when I get other planes, you shall have your fill of bombing and fighting, Mr. Hawkins. But not now."

" As you say, sir," said Billy, saluting, then he clambered into his seat. The Dolphin's great engine roared, she sped across the sun-scorched grass, leaped into the air, and flew swiftly across the forests towards the west.

" There is Tobosa," said the Professor, and Billy, glancing down, saw half a dozen tall, skeleton-like derricks sticking up out of the plain, and around them a huddle of scrappy-looking buildings roofed with galvanised iron, sheds and tents. A made road ran like a brown riband across the plain and continued beyond it into the distant hills.

Billy nodded. " So that's where they've struck the oil?" he remarked. " And I suppose those tents are occupied by Castro's crew. Yes, I can see guns and quite a lot of cars. I had better keep clear, hadn't I?" he added reluctantly.

" No, you can go right over the place," replied Cottle, " but go high."

Billy was astonished, but did as he was told, and the Dolphin was somewhere about the ten-thousand-foot level when she arrived above the new oil wells.

" Circle a bit, Billy," said Cottle, who was gazing downwards.

As he banked, Billy had a chance of looking

down. He gasped. "Great snakes, but if that isn't a gun I'll eat it, Professor!" he exclaimed.

"It's an anti-aircraft right enough, Billy," replied Cottle quietly. "That was what I wanted to see."

"But why in sense don't the beggars use it? We are within range, all right."

"That's the question I am asking myself," replied the other. "I wish they would use it, Billy."

Billy stared. "Gee, but I'm not hankering after any of that stuff," he said. "What's the great idea, Professor?"

"I wish I knew, my boy," answered Cottle. "You can shove on, now. Keep over the road, and let's see what is on the other side of those hills."

The hills, as Cottle called them, were a range of very respectable mountains which barred the horizon to the west. They were not snow-clad peaks or anything of that kind, but rather a gigantic slope climbing to an almost level table-land.

As the plane swept onwards her passengers could see the road running endlessly upwards. It was a mere track cut through the scrub which covered the sides of the great hill. Miles away up from Tobosa a small party of men with pack mules were coming down the hill. They saw or heard the plane, and at once dived into the scrub and hid themselves.

"I wish we had what those mules are carrying," said Cottle.

" What is it?" asked Billy eagerly.

" Green gold, I fancy," was the answer, and Billy felt a thrill run through him, for it seemed to him that they were at last approaching the goal of their long journey. Flinging the miles behind her, the Dolphin was presently above the range, and under her lay a tableland many miles in width, all covered with the same wiry scrub.

" Regular desert," said Billy, glancing down. " I say, Professor, that road must have taken a bit of making."

" All Castro's work," replied Cottle meaningly. " It must lead straight to Sanat."

" Sanat—the lost city, you mean?" exclaimed Billy.

" That is what I believe, Billy. Sanat means ' Eternal,' and I think it likely that presently you and I may be looking down upon what are perhaps the oldest buildings which remain upon the face of this planet."

" What—here in South America?"

" Just so. Part of South America, I grant you, is very new. The Andes, for instance, are still rising. But here we have below us land which has been above the sea for millions of years. From information given me by one of the best-known explorers, a former colonel in the Gunners, I believe that this is a part of the ancient Atlantean Continent, which remained when the great earthquakes and eruptions sank the rest into the depths of the ocean. And Sanat, if it survives, must be the remains of one of those vast Atlantean cities of which the Egyptian priests told the Greek, Plato, more than two thousand years ago."

"This is frightfully exciting," cried Billy. "And this is where Castro gets his green gold?"

"That is what I am hoping——" Cottle broke off short. "Look!" he exclaimed, pointing. Billy looked, and this is what he saw.

Miles ahead, yet becoming clearer every moment, was a vast pit or crater. It was many hundreds of feet in depth and was ringed by cliffs of broken rock which dropped in a series of giant steps to a great stretch of level ground, the vivid green of which was in startling contrast to the dull greyish tint of the scrub which covered the surrounding desert. Pools of water, blue as the sky above, dotted this wide plain, and near the centre was visible a mass of buildings covering many acres.

"Sanat! Is that Sanat?" demanded Billy.

"I have not much doubt about it," replied Cottle.

Billy watched with breathless interest as the Dolphin swept towards the mysterious crater. Another ten minutes and they were above it.

Billy whistled softly. "Look at the size of it, Professor!" he gasped. "Why, those little ponds are big lakes. And the city! It's miles across. Shall I drop a bit? Even Castro can hardly have got guns up here."

"No," replied Cottle. "I don't suppose that he has guns, Billy. You can drop a little, but don't go too close."

Billy gave his companion a quick glance. "I'll

keep high enough to be safe from rifle fire or flaming onions or any jape of that sort," he said quietly. " You'll take notes, sir, won't you?"

The Dolphin swung out high over the great step-like cliffs which ringed the valley, and Billy saw that the valley itself was oval in shape, some seven or eight miles long and perhaps five wide. The bottom seemed almost level, and a small river, breaking out of the cliffs on the north, fed the lakes, of which there were three, and disappeared into a tunnel at the south-west end.

But it was the city which fixed Billy's attention; and certainly no stranger buildings have ever been seen by twentieth-century eyes. In the centre was an enormous square, the four sides of which seemed to face the cardinal points of the compass. In the middle of the square was a great pyramid-shaped erection, with a flat top on which stood a stone statue representing a giant man. One arm was outstretched and pointing towards the north, but the plane was still too high to make out details. The eastern side of the square was occupied by a vast temple-like building made of gigantic blocks of stone. Part of the roof had fallen in, but Billy could see that the front was richly sculptured.

What puzzled him most, however, were the houses, most of which were shaped like great beehives, and seemed to have no doors or windows. " Who on earth could have lived there?" he demanded of Cottle. " Were they all blind or what?"

Cottle did not answer, and Billy, looking at

him again, was struck by his peculiar expression. His lips were tight set, and his face paler than usual, while his intensely blue eyes were searching the scene below with an extraordinarily intent gaze.

"Can you see anything, Billy?" he asked sharply.

"Not a soul," began Billy, then corrected himself. "Yes, I can. There's a chap in the shadow there under the temple portico. What's he doing? Looks to me as if he was working a movie camera."

"Turn! Bank! Quick as you can, Billy," cried Cottle with such intensity that the words seemed to bite into Billy's brain. He obeyed instantly and the great machine came round at a tremendously steep angle.

"What's the matter?" began Billy, and, as the words left his lips, the engine's roar ceased with a suddenness that gave Billy a dazed feeling. "What in sense is up?" he gasped, his fingers busy with the controls.

"It's no use, Billy," said Cottle grimly. "You will not get her going again. Make the best landing you can. That is all that there is left to be done."

CHAPTER THIRTEEN

A CITY OF THE DEAD

It was more by instinct than any conscious effort that Billy straightened out the Dolphin and brought her down. Fortunately there was plenty of room in the great square, and fortunately, too, the surface of the ground was fairly smooth. He made an almost perfect landing and, swinging the plane round, brought her to rest close under the huge monument in the centre of the square.

Billy's head was still spinning with the suddenness of it all. A few seconds before they had been sailing serenely high above the ruined city, and now, for no reason that he could understand, they were on the ground and helpless. He looked round. The man with the camera, or whatever his machine had been, was no longer visible. The great square, ablaze with tropical sunshine, seemed entirely deserted. He and Cottle were alone in a city of the dead.

His eyes sought Cottle's. " What is it, sir? What's happened?" Cottle's fine face was hard as stone. " You saw as much as I did," he answered curtly.

" I saw a dago pointing a camera-thing at us." He stopped short, and a look of something like horror crossed his face. " A ray—a death ray! Was that it, Professor?"

"That was it, Billy," replied Cottle. "The moment I saw the man pointing his machine at us I suspected what he was after, and from the way in which the engine stopped there can't be much doubt that they were using some ray which directly affected our magneto."

"But what's the great idea?" demanded Billy, who was beginning to recover himself. "They've got us down, but unless their ray is good against our machine-guns it's not going to help them a lot." While he spoke, Billy's fingers were busy with the mechanism of his machine-gun, making sure that the cartridge clips were in position and the gun itself ready to swing into position.

But it was one thing to make the gun ready, quite another to find anything to use it against. After a moment or two Billy spoke again:

"Professor, you handle the gun while I look at the engine. I don't know whether there's a dog's chance of finding the trouble and repairing it, but if there is a chance, we mustn't waste it."

"Try if you like, Billy," said Cottle, "but I'm very much afraid you will do no good. If I'm not greatly mistaken you'll find your magneto completely messed up."

He slipped into Billy's place, and Billy at once tackled the engine. Within less than three minutes Cottle heard him give an angry grunt.

"Am I right?" asked the Professor.

"You're right," said Billy grimly. "The magneto is burnt out, and the Dolphin won't fly again until we can fit a new one."

" I take it that's a longish job?" said Cottle.

" A very long job, I'm afraid," said Billy dolefully, " and for all I know that beastly ray has ruined our spare as well as the one which was in use. Do you see any sign of our friend with the ray-camera?"

" If I had I should have shot first and told you afterwards," responded Cottle.

" What's their game?" demanded Billy.

" I'm not too sure," Cottle answered, " but I rather think they're trying to put the wind up us."

" I don't know about trying to put the wind up us," said Billy, " but I do know that if we stick here much longer we shall get the skin scorched off us."

" It's certainly hot, Billy," agreed Cottle, " but I don't see any remedy for that. These people, whoever they are, are laying for us, and our one chance is to keep our fingers on the trigger—so to speak."

" Fancy the beggars having the ray!" groaned Billy. " Who'd have dreamed of that sort of thing in this weird old ruined town hundreds of miles from anywhere?"

" I will admit it was a shock," said Cottle gravely; " the more so because, although a number of so-called death rays have been invented, I myself was not aware of anything that would work at such a distance or with such power. I shall be interested to know how it does work."

Billy shrugged. " I should be a jolly sight

more interested to see my engines working again, Professor. Looks to me as if we were in an uncommonly tight place. And what makes it all the worse is that we don't seem to know whom we are up against."

"There is not much doubt about that," replied Cottle. "This is Castro's scheme. He is probably the only one out of the rebel gang who has the brains for such a stunt of this sort."

"You are perfectly right, Professor." The words, spoken in English, made Billy fairly jump, while even Cottle started sharply. No wonder, for they were not shouted but merely spoken in quite an ordinary voice, so that it sounded as though the speaker must be standing alongside the plane. Yet, as before, there was no living being within sight.

"Who is it? Where is he?" gasped Billy.

"It is General Castro who speaks," came the answer in the same excellent English. "As for where he is—that I have no intention of divulging until I know upon what terms we stand. The machine-gun is, I happen to know, a Madsen, and my men do not wish to lose their leader any more than I desire to lose my life."

Billy's eyes were wide as he turned to Cottle. "Can you tell where he is?" he whispered.

Cottle shook his head. "No," he answered in an equally low voice; "but he is using a voice projector, and is catching our voices by a somewhat similar device."

"What happens now, then? Are you going to talk to him?" asked Billy.

Before the Professor could answer they heard Castro's voice again. "I cannot hear you when you whisper," he stated; "so if you wish to consult between yourselves you are safe in doing so. But if you speak in an ordinary voice I can hear you almost as plainly as you can hear me."

"We shall have to make terms, I suppose, Billy," whispered Cottle.

"I suppose we shall," replied Billy reluctantly; "but—but what about the bus? We can't let Castro get his hands on her."

"You mean we should destroy her?"

Billy gulped. "N-nothing else for it, is there?" he answered.

Cottle considered. "I don't think we will do that, Billy," he said gravely. "If we burn her we cut off our last chance of either getting away or making good."

"All right," whispered Billy. "Then tell the beggar to come out into the open and let us hear what he has to say."

Cottle raised his voice. "We wish to parley," he stated.

"Then have I your word as English gentlemen that you will not shoot if I show myself?" demanded the unseen Castro.

"Of course," replied Cottle coolly, and at that a man stepped out from under the dark shadow of the temple portico opposite.

"You had better come this way," he remarked. "The heat in the square is too great for comfort, and you will find it much pleasanter in the shade of this old building. You need not trouble about the aeroplane which will not be interfered with by any of my people.''

'' Do we trust him, Professor?'' whispered Billy.

'' I wish I knew,'' replied Cottle ruefully. '' Unluckily, he is too far away at present for me to use my faculty of thought reading. But I think that we shall have to take his word.''

'' All right, sir,'' said Billy. '' I don't mind telling you that my brain feels as if it were boiling.''

'' We will come across,'' said Cottle to Castro as he stepped out of the plane and, followed by Billy, walked quietly across the great square. Castro waited under the massive portico and not another soul. Yet Billy had the feeling that unseen eyes were watching him and his companion.

Castro himself came down the steps and advanced to meet them, and Billy saw at once that the rebel leader was a very different type of man from those of his followers whom he had already met. He was comparatively tall and very powerfully built, with square shoulders and an upright carriage. He looked to be about forty years of age. His skin was olive in colour and his eyes inscrutably black, while he wore his dark hair cropped short. He was dressed in a dark-blue uniform, very well made, but with none of the gold lace of which his followers were so fond.

He bowed gravely as the others came up. '' This way, please,'' he said. He led them up a flight of enormous stone steps and across the portico, through an arched entrance into a chamber which, by contrast, seemed almost dark. But the coolness was delicious after the fierce sun glare in the square. "Sit down," he said hospitably, pointing to some canvas chairs which were arranged around a camp table. "You will allow me to offer you something to drink."

Without waiting for their answer he poured some lime juice from a bottle into three glasses, and filled them up with soda water. "I will take the third glass, if you will help yourselves," he said politely, and even Cottle could not well refuse.

Billy's eyes were getting accustomed to the dim light and, glancing round, he saw that monstrous stone carvings stood out weirdly from the walls.

"A wonderful place," said Castro. "The most wonderful ruins in the world, I believe. You must examine them after we have had our little talk." He fixed his dark eyes on Cottle. "It gave you a shock to be brought down like that, Señor Professor," he said.

"I admit it," replied Cottle; "but you would not have succeeded if your spy had not got at the plane before we left Las Cruces."

General Castro merely smiled. "Ah, so you realise that." He shrugged his shoulders. "All part of the game, Señor Cottle. You cannot complain, for you must remember that you were not asked to butt in."

"There you are wrong," replied Cottle. "President Tenorio is a very old friend of mine, and my help was especially requested by him. But do not let us indulge in recriminations. For the moment you have the better of us, and now I wish to know where we stand."

"For the moment?" repeated Castro. "Surely that is understating the case, señor. You must admit that you are completely in my power. But I do not want to be unpleasant," he added hastily. "If I had, I could have turned machine-guns upon you in the square and shot you to pieces."

Cottle's sky-blue eyes gleamed oddly. "Yes, if you have the guns here, Señor Castro," he answered smoothly.

Castro showed his white teeth in an unpleasant smile. "I have them all right, Professor. Later, if necessary, you shall see them. But, as I have said before, I am anxious not to quarrel, especially with a gentleman for whose knowledge I have so great a respect as I have for yours. Now, please listen to me. Although this is the first time that we have met, Professor, this is not the first time that we have clashed. I would like to know why you have made it your business to oppose me?"

"I have told you," said Cottle. "I am a friend of President Tenorio who I know has been a good ruler of San Lucar, and I have no intention of seeing the country handed over to those whose one idea is to fill their pockets."

Castro's lips tightened. "You are frank, at any rate, Professor. Let us come down to what my American friends call brass tacks. Are you and Mr. Hawkins willing to purchase your freedom by doing me a service?"

"I hope you are not asking us to come in with you," said Cottle grimly.

"Certainly not. This is what I require. I have a case, a small but very valuable case, which I want transferred from Ambala here to Tobosa. Will you take it in your plane, and at the same time give me a passage?" Billy was about to speak, but Castro raised his hand. "You have a spare magneto, and you will find it quite safe. You can, I feel sure, fit it before dark."

"Yes, I can do that," said Billy

"Then will you do as I ask?"

"Is that all?" demanded Cottle.

"Yes, that is all, except, of course, that I shall require your word that you will at once leave San Lucar and take no further part against me. Do not answer in a hurry. Take a few minutes to think over the matter, and, meantime, I will go out about some business of my own."

He got up quickly and went out, and until his footsteps had died away, there was complete silence in the great, dusky room. Then Billy spoke. "What do you think, Professor? What is he after? Can we depened on him?"

Cottle shrugged his shoulders. "He's bad medicine, Billy," he answered.

"What do you mean? Is he playing some dirty game on us?"

"It is very difficult for me to say, Billy,"

replied the other gravely. " Do you know what
my main impression is about him?"

" What is it?" demanded Billy.

" That he is scared—badly scared."

" What of?"

" I have no idea at all. But that Castro is
frightened and very seriously frightened—of that
I have no doubt whatever."

CHAPTER FOURTEEN

HOLE IN THE WALL

BILLY sat frowning. " Yes, I begin to see, Professor. Castro wants to get away from here and
that's why he's so civil to us. But what is in this
case he talks about?"

" Something very valuable, Billy. More of
the gold that he has been looting here, I expect."

Billy considered again. " Then it looks as if
some of his own people were on his trail. Yet,
after all, he must have been up here a goodish
time, for he must have been getting the gold for
months past."

" Certainly he has been getting it for a long
time past," said Cottle. " I had that specimen
in England nearly three months ago. The whole
thing is an absolute puzzle."

Billy ran his fingers through his hair. " A
puzzle we haven't time to solve," he answered.
" Castro will be back just now. What are we

going to say to him? Surely we are not going to pull his chestnuts out of the fire for him."

That is, of course, out of the question," agreed Cottle. " Yet if we refuse, you may take it that he will turn nasty."

Billy shrugged again. " Ugly as sin, I expect. Well, it can't be helped. By jove, here he is! You tackle him, Professor. I back you to the limit."

As Billy spoke Castro came in again, and Billy, watching him keenly saw that Cottle was right. In spite of his impassive face the rebel leader was certainly uneasy. " Well," he said, addressing Cottle. " Do you agree to my proposal?"

" I want to know a little more about it first," said Cottle crisply. " This case you speak of— I take it that it contains more of the sinews of war?"

Castro's face hardened. " That is a question which I decline to answer. I consider that I am treating you in a most generous manner. Sensible men would jump at such a chance."

Cottle's face did not change. " That is not quite as it appears to me, Señor Castro. We are to help you to remove this gold which is to be used against President Tenorio, and which, it is evident, you very badly want moved. Then, when we arrive at Tobosa, you promise to turn us loose on getting our word that we leave the country. But even if you are willing to let us go, how do we know that your precious allies will share your views?"

Castro's whole expression altered, and for an instant Billy got a glimpse of the real man, a glimpse which gave him a nasty shock.

"I have stated my terms," he said harshly. "You can take them or leave them. But if you refuse to accept them I think you will shortly be very sorry."

"Threats cut no ice," returned Cottle as coolly as ever, "and I tell you quite definitely that we refuse to do as you suggest."

Castro's right hand flashed to his pocket, and came out grasping an automatic, but Cottle was already on his feet, and his long arm, shooting out across the table, caught Castro by the left wrist and jerked him round. The pistol cracked, but the bullet buried itself in the ceiling, bringing down a spatter of stone splinters.

Quick as lightning, Billy leapt round behind Castro, and before the man could fire again, had wrenched the pistol from him. The table and glasses went flying as Cottle closed with Castro.

Castro was the heavier of the two, but Cottle's wiry strength was too much for him, and closing, he tripped him and the two went down together on the stone floor. Billy had whipped out a handkerchief, and was about to help Cottle tie up their prisoner, when a clatter of boots on stone reached his ears, and he swung round just in time to see half a dozen ragged-looking ruffians, armed with knives, come charging through the door. Whipping round, he raised Castro's pistol. "Stop!" he shouted. "The first of you who moves get it in the neck!"

His curt command had its effect. The bunch of dagoes pulled up short in the doorway, and stood scowling and glaring at the white boy who faced them so boldly.

" Can you handle Castro, Professor?" asked Billy, without looking round.

" Yes; I have him safely," was the answer.

" That's a good job, for it strikes me he's the only thing we've got to bargain with."

" They are not beauties, that's one thing sure," agreed Cottle, who had now succeeded in pinning Castro so that he was quite helpless. " Can you chase them off, Billy?"

Billy took a step forward.

" Vamose!" he ordered. " Clear out of this, the lot of you!"

The men glared back at him, but did not offer to move. On the contrary, they growled in their throats and looked as threatening as a pack of wolves.

" They don't scare worth a cent, Professor," said Billy. " And if they start shooting it's going to be mighty awkward. I can plug two or three, but there's quite a crowd outside and more coming, by the look of it." Cottle, who by this time had managed to tie Castro's wrists behind him, dragged the rebel leader to his feet. " They'll hardly start shooting, for if they do they'll slay their own Castro," he observed. He spoke to Castro. " Hadn't you better order your chaps to get outside?" he suggested.

" I shall do nothing of the sort," retorted Castro. " On the contrary, if you have any sense at all, you will realise that you are in a perfectly hopeless position, and surrender. My offer is still open.''

'' Very kind of you, I'm sure,'' returned Cottle equably; '' but once I have turned a thing down I am not accustomed to changing my mind. As for our position being hopeless, I do not agree with you, for so long as you are our prisoner we hold the winning cards.''

'' And what are you going to do with me?'' sneered Castro. '' You can hold me here for an hour, or even perhaps longer, but you cannot leave the place, and even if you tried to, you would be shot down before you had gone ten steps.''

'' Getting peevish, aren't you?'' suggested Billy, but though he spoke lightly he was not happy. In his heart he knew that Castro was right. It was only a question of time before the fellows made a rush, and although, as he had said, he could shoot two or three, the end would come quickly.

He glanced round the room, wondering if there was any other way of getting out. High in the outer wall was an opening, a sort of glassless window, but it was nearly twenty feet from the ground, and plainly out of reach except with a ladder. For the rest there appeared nothing but the door which was blocked by Castro's un-washed soldiery.

And then, just as Billy's glance slid sideways along the inner wall of the great room, it seemed to him that he caught a movement. Billy hardly dared to take his eyes off the pack of ruffians in front, for he knew that if he did so they would rush, yet he did glance once more in the direction of the stealthy movement. The movement had ceased, yet if Billy was not dreaming there, under a great mass of carving which stood out at a man's height from the floor, was a small patch of blackness. An opening in the wall.

Hardly able to believe his eyes, he took one more glance, and now he was sure. How it had happened—that was beyond telling—but without the slightest doubt the opening did exist. Had Cottle seen it?—that was the great question, but apparently he had not, and the question was, how to tell him without informing their enemies. Castro spoke English, so it was no use speaking in that language, and Billy guessed that he probably knew French as well. For an instant Billy racked his brain for any way of communication, then there flickered through his memory some old tags of Latin learned at school. " Portus, Professor," he said; " portus in muro—door in wall "—that was as far as he could get, for he could not remember the word for open.

There was a moment's pause, then Cottle spoke. " I get you," he answered coolly. " Wait a jiffy."

Billy would have given worlds to know what the Professor was doing or what plan he was making, but he dared not take his eyes off those restless, snarling wolves at the outer door.

Of a sudden Cottle made a swift motion and something passed high in the air over Billy's head and fell with a crisp tinkle on the stone floor between Billy and the gang. In an instant a great cloud of smoke, black as soot, rolled up, completely hiding all that side of the room. " Now!" snapped Cottle, and grabbing Castro by the scruff of his neck rushed him across towards the opening. As Billy followed Hades broke loose. Half a dozen rifles spoke at once, the din of the firing in that confined space being simply deafening. Then figures came leaping through the mounting gloom.

Billy kept his head. He fired and fired again, and saw the first two of the dagoes reel back and crash to the floor. " All right!" came Cottle's voice from the direction of the door, and Billy simply leaped after him. But as he leapt, one of Castro's men, charging out of the gloom, met him full and the shock sent him reeling. He felt the man's great hand grasping at his throat, and, lifting the pistol, pulled the trigger again. The hammer snapped harmlessly, and before he could fire again he was flung backwards and, losing his balance, went crashing to the floor.

Billy struggled and writhed, but the great hand that clutched his throat was shutting off his breath. His head began to swim and stars of light danced and spun before his eyes.

With a last desperate effort he drew up both legs and kicked out with all his force. His feet got the dago in the stomach and with a grunting groan the man went limp. In a flash Billy had wrenched himself away, rolled over and staggered to his feet. Through the smoke he caught a vague glimpse of one of the monstrous carvings on the left-hand wall. He flung himself towards it and heard Cottle call: " Billy! Billy, where are you?"

" Here!" he gasped.

" This way," came Cottle's voice. " Here's the door!"

Another of the dagoes came at Billy, swinging at him with the butt of his rifle, but before the blow could land, the man shrieked and went over backwards for Cottle had caught him from behind by one ankle. Billy flung himself over the man's prostrate body, found himself at the mouth of the entrance and instantly hurled himself through.

" Quickly!" snapped Cottle. " Get behind me and I'll shut it." Billy flung himself down. Next instant the door swung to, closing with an echoing slam, and instantly all sounds from the temple chamber were cut off.

" Where are we?" asked Billy hoarsely.

" I've no more notion than you, but, anyhow, we're out of the reach of those swine," answered Cottle. " And we have Castro, which is all to the good. . . Wait a moment, I have matches somewhere."

He found the box, but before he could strike one Billy called out: " Steady! Here's a light coming."

Sure enough a glow like that of an electric torch, but softer and more phosphorescent in character, had appeared behind them and was coming towards them, and Billy and Cottle both turned sharply towards it. "What the mischief is it?" demanded Billy. "If it's more of the dagoes we're done in, Professor."

"It's no dago, it's a boy," Cottle answered. "A boy? Yes—and white, too." Almost paralysed with astonishment, the two stared at the newcomer who came steadily up towards them. Up, because the passage, which was built of the same giant masonry as the rest of the temple, sloped steeply upwards. As the stranger drew nearer, Billy saw that he was no boy but a grown man. He was, however, not more than five feet in height, yet very well built and proportioned.

His skin was white as Billy's own, he had blue eyes and fair hair. He was dressed in a cotton tunic, curiously embroidered, wore sandals, and had at his side a short sword with a cross handle. Billy stared at him in amazement.

Small as the newcomer was, there was nothing weak or feeble about him. On the other hand, he had the air of knowing just what he wanted and—so Billy thought—of getting it. He held himself very straight, and, as he came to a stop in front of the two Englishmen, looked them full in the face. Then he glanced at Castro, and a look of utter contempt and loathing crossed his face. He spoke to Cottle, but the language he used was one of which neither Cottle nor Billy could make anything.

Cottle answered in Spanish. "I am sorry, but I do not understand you," he said courteously.

The little man frowned. " Why do you, who are white like myself, speak in the language of our enemies?" he demanded in good Spanish.

" We are English," explained Cottle.

" English," repeated the other, evidently puzzled. Then he looked at Castro who leaned sulkily against the wall, with his hands tied behind him. " But you are not friends of this man?"

" Far from it," said Cottle. " We are the allies of this man's enemies. He is a rebel who is trying to destroy the State of San Lucar."

" How came you here?" questioned the little man.

Cottle explained, and when he spoke of the aeroplane, the other's face lighted up with a look of extraordinary interest. " So there are again flying machines in the world," he exclaimed.

" Again!" repeated Billy, who knew enough Spanish to understand what was being said. " What does he mean, Professor?"

Cottle's blue eyes were blazing with excitement and interest. " I am not sure, Billy, but I believe we are on the edge of something pretty big. If I am not mistaken, our friend here is of the Chiapas, a race which was in existence when the Spaniards first came, but which has long been believed to be extinct." He turned to the little man. " Señor, you are of the Chiapas?" he questioned eagerly.

The other drew himself up. " I am Copan, chief of the remnant of that race," he answered; " but how knew you of the Chiapas?"

Before Cottle could reply there came a heavy thudding sound. Billy started. "Those dagoes have found the door," he exclaimed. "They're trying to break it down."

Cottle explained to Copan, but the latter merely smiled. "It will take more than hammers to break through," he said. "Yet, if they use the fire powder, it is possible that they may succeed, nor is there need to run risks. Follow me and I will lead you to a place of safety."

He turned and led the way back down the passage which sloped away apparently into the bowels of the earth. With Castro between them, Cottle and Billy followed. Castro's dark face was livid with anger—and perhaps fear—but he was quite helpless. They went no more than about a hundred yards, when Copan stopped short, and with his sword-hilt, struck upon the wall. To all appearances this part of the wall was just like any of the rest, built of the same huge stones accurately cut and fitted. But within a few moments of Copan's knock there came a slight grating sound and a section of the wall, some six feet high by three feet wide, swung inwards on invisible hinges.

Copan waited until the door had been quite lifted, then led the way through, and they found themselves in a second passage. To right and left of the entrances were deep recesses, in one of which stood a man of type similar to Copan, who worked the door by means of a big, bronze-handled lever.

On and on they went until Billy began to wonder whether they would ever get to the end of this amazing corridor, and if they would ever see daylight again. At last he thought he saw light in the distance.

" See it, Professor?" he asked.

" Yes; but it's not daylight, Billy. It's too blue." Slowly the light increased, then of a sudden the echoes altered and the little party stepped out of the tunnel into a rock chamber of such size that it looked like the interior of a great cathedral, and Billy, pulling up short, stared at the strange scene which lay before him.

CHAPTER FIFTEEN

ADDED DANGER

THE lights—they were the first thing that Billy stared at. Set high in the wall at regular intervals, they glowed with a soft blue radiance, indescribably beautiful. At first sight Billy thought they were electric, but a second look showed that they were similar to that which Copan carried—that is, a sort of brillant phosphorescence.

But there was no time to speculate on their nature for it was what they showed which gave Billy and Cottle most cause for amazement. From among the tremendous columns which supported the roof of the vast underground hall people were approaching—numbers of them, both men and women—and all, like Copan, white skinned, fair-haired and blue-eyed. All were dressed in linen tunics similar to that which Copan wore, but the women wore necklaces and bracelets, and from Billy's lips came instinctively the two words: " Green gold."

" Green gold, all right, Billy," repeated Cottle, then Copan stopped, and his people surrounded him and the others.

Copan spoke to them in their own language, and his voice rang high and clear. He pointed first to Cottle and Billy and the people cheered— then to Castro, and there was no mistaking the note of threat in their voices. Castro heard it, too, and his dark face went the colour of ashes.

" I say, Professor, we'll have to look out," said Billy in a low voice. " For two pins they'd tear Castro to pieces."

" Don't know that I wonder at it," replied Cottle dryly. " Still, we can't have that. I'll just give Copan the tip."

He stepped up to Copan and spoke to him in whispered Spanish, and Copan, though at first he frowned, presently nodded. " It's all right, Billy," said Cottle. " Copan has promised to keep him safe. I've told him that Castro is too valuable as a hostage to risk, and Copan is going to shut him up somewhere in safety."

" Are you sure he will?" asked Billy rather anxiously.

" Quite sure," Cottle answered gravely.

" Castro doesn't seem to think so," grinned

Billy as the rebel leader was led away. "He's scared stiff."

"Do him good," growled Cottle. "And yet between you and me he's no worse scared now than he was when we first met in the upper cave. There's something queer about all this."

"Queer! That's a mild word," returned Billy.

Before he could say more, Copan was asking them to accompany him. He led them across the cave, and as they approached the opposite wall, they saw a number of arched doorways, to one of which Copan took them. The door was covered by a curtain which Copan lifted. "This will be your apartment, señores, while you honour us with your company."

"What a top-hole place!" exclaimed Billy. "I say, Professor, I never had a room like this before!"

"It is rather wonderful," agreed Cottle as he looked round.

One of the blue lights showed them a large square room hewn in the living rock. On one side was a raised platform on which were two cot-like beds. The other furniture consisted of a table of dark wood curiously carved, and two chairs which were oddly like those found in Egyptian tombs. On the other side of the room was a deep pool of beautifully clear water, fed by a spout cut in the wall.

"What a bath!" cried Billy in such delight that even Copan smiled.

"I am pleased that you like it," he said.

" After you have bathed, food will be brought to you."

He was hardly outside before Billy was peeling off his clothes. Next moment he and Cottle were both in the crystal pool, diving, swimming and splashing. After the fierce heat of the square and the sultry air of the passages the water was deliciously cool and bracing, and Billy would have stayed in an hour if Cottle had not ordered him to come out.

They were hardly finished dressing before Copan returned and with him a man carrying a tray which was cut into sections by cross-pieces. In the sections was food of different kinds. In one, maize cakes; in another, baked yams, and, in a third, beans baked with some sort of meat. Plain food, but Billy was starving, and the smell of it was excellent. Cottle begged Copan to eat with them, and Copan, though he excused himself from eating, sat down, evidently quite ready to talk.

Cottle asked him about his people and the other answered frankly. " We have lived here always," he said. " Before ever the Incas settled in the West this city of Sanat was old. The Incas never conquered us, nor did the Spaniards, for the swamps on one side and the desert on the other have protected us."

" Then how is it that your great city has fallen to ruin?" questioned Cottle.

" It was the tremblor, señor," Copan answered. " The Earth God shook the mountains and much of the city fell. The ground cracked and the river fell through. Many died of thirst and others of famine and of disease."

" But you have plenty of water now," exclaimed Billy.

" True, my friend," said Copan. " After many years the Earth God shook the ground again and the waters came back to us. But by that time there were few left, and never have we returned to our former power and glory."

" I understand," said Cottle gently, " but tell me, why have you gone underground like this, Copan?"

Copan did not answer at once, and Billy saw his face change. Cottle leaned forward. " Tell me, Copan, has it anything to do with the fear that has fallen upon Castro?"

Copan looked up sharply. " How knowest thou that the fear is upon Castro?" he asked. Cottle did not answer, and Copan, after gazing at him for a few moments, nodded. " I understand," he said gravely. " Thou hast the inner sense."

" Then I am right," said Cottle.

" Thou art right, my lord," said Copan. " The fear that is upon Castro is upon all of us also."

Cottle waited in silence. Billy leaned forward. At last Copan spoke. " The Araks," he said in a voice that was little more than a whisper. " The Araks are upon us."

" The Araks," repeated Billy. " Who the mischief are the Araks?"

" They are devils, señor. The enemies of God and man."

" Sounds cheerful," grunted Billy, and turned to Cottle. " Have you ever heard of them, Professor?"

" Yes, Billy. You will find mention of them in the early Portuguese records." He paused. " They are said to be the remnants of a savage tribe which once occupied a large part of inner Brazil, but were mostly destroyed by the great Carib invasion from the north. They are hairy, clay-coloured men of enormous strength, cannibals, and more savage than wild beasts. They have powers of scent equal to those of a hunting dog, and, it is said, are nyctalops—that is, able to see like cats in the dark."

Billy whistled softly. " Nice crowd to be up against," he remarked. " But I don't quite get the hang of it. Why are they on the war-path now?"

Copan answered. " The Gods forgive us, señor! We sent for them."

" You sent for them?" exclaimed Cottle. " Yes, I see. You would hide while they wiped out Castro and his crew."

" Thou hast guessed right," said Copan gravely.

" But when are they coming?" demanded Billy sharply.

" Soon, señor," Copan answered. " It may be this very night."

Billy turned to Cottle. " The plane!" he

exclaimed. " We've got to save her. Ask Copan if there is any way of doing it."

Cottle put the question, but Copan shook his head. " I see no way, señor. True, the Araks travel only in the darkness, but in the day Castro's men guard the Place of the Man who Points."

Billy's lips tightened. " Professor, if we lose the plane we are done in. I don't care what the risks are; somehow we have to save the Dolphin."

" You are right, Billy," Cottle answered. " Yet on the face of it I can't see any way of saving her. As you said yourself, it will take a couple of hours to put her other magneto in place, and you need daylight to do it. Yet obviously we cannot go up to the Square in daylight."

" Then we must wait for night," said Billy, and chance the niggers. Ask Copan if there is any safe way up."

Cottle questioned the little chief, and, after a few moments' talk, turned again to Billy. " Yes, Billy, there is a way up—a secret way. What is more, Copan tells me that there is a spot where it might be possible to hide the plane. A place just outside the Square. If we could only manage to push her into this place we might have the chance of repairing her in safety."

Billy's face cleared. " Good business!" he exclaimed. " Then the sooner we fix up the better, for it's four now, and the sun will be down in two hours. Ask Copan to show us the way."

" I will accompany you, señores," said the little chief quietly.

He got up at once and they followed him out of the rock chamber, across the great pillared hall towards an arched entrance at the far side.

In front was a tunnel cut through the living rock, but not lighted. There was no need, for at the far end, only fifty paces away, daylight showed. Not bright sunlight, but a twilight gleam which at first puzzled Billy. But when he reached the end of the tunnel he understood, for he found himself on a narrow gallery cut in the face of a sheer cliff, and opposite, only fifty feet away, was also cliff. Beneath was a great rift, so deep, so dark, that the eye could not penetrate its tremendous depths. " It was the tremblor," Copan explained. " The Earth God was angry with us Chiapas and split the city."

" Some split," agreed Billy softly.

Copan turned to the right and led the way along the gallery. There was no parapet or hand-rail—nothing between them and the monstrous depths which yawned below. And the ledge was narrow, nowhere more than six feet in width, and in some places only half as much. The ledge sloped steadily upwards at a gentle angle, then ended in another tunnel which burrowed deep into the right-hand cliff. Copan took his lamp from a pocket in his tunic and led the way.

This tunnel seemed endless but at last they found themselves once more in a rock chamber, from which there did not seem any way out. Copan, however, went straight ahead and the others followed. Presently Copan's light showed a great beam projecting from the wall at a height of about four feet from the floor. It was some ten feet long, and its outer end was provided with a sort of huge spoon. Copan went straight up to it and, first handing his lamp to Billy, picked up some smooth boulders which lay by the wall and began piling them into the spoon.

"A counterpoise, Billy," said Cottle with a flash of interest in his vividly blue eyes. As he spoke there was a very faint creaking sound, the beam dipped and a stone shield in the wall moved slowly upwards, leaving a hole about three feet by two through which daylight broke into the cavern.

Copan stepped forward and glanced through, then, making a sign for silence, beckoned the others to approach. To his amazement, Billy found himself almost within touching distance of his beloved Dolphin. The opening from which he was looking out was in the base of the giant monument which stood in the centre of the Square. The sun was low, and the shadow of the great boulder and of the colossal statue on its summit fell across the plane.

"What luck!" gasped Billy. "And not even a guard over her. I say, Professor, what price slipping through and getting to work at once?"

But Cottle caught him by the arm and drew him back. "Don't be a fool, Billy," he said sharply. "Remember Castro's men are in the temple. We must wait here until dark before we can get to work. Luckily the moon does not rise until past midnight.''

'' I suppose you are right,'' said Billy reluctantly as he drew back. Then Copan unloaded the stones from the counterpoise, the stone shutter slipped back into place, and by the blue light of Copan's lamp the three set themselves to wait for darkness.

The waiting was not so bad as it might have been, for Copan was thrilled at sight of the plane, and told his two hearers that in the old days, when the Chiapas had first built Sanat, they too had had flying machines.

'' How do you know?'' demanded Billy.

'' We have pictures of them, señores,'' said Copan simply.

Billy began to ask all sorts of questions, and as Copan talked his wonder deepened. For he soon came to realise that Copan's people were indeed the relics of a race who had known things which no twentieth-century scientist had discovered. One was cold light as shown in the torch which Copan carried, another was a method of making bronze tools which were as hard as the best Sheffield steel. Billy and Copan were still deep in discussion when Cottle looked at his wrist-watch. '' Nearly seven, Billy,'' he said. '' It will be as dark as it is ever going to be. There is no time to waste.''

Copan agreed, the stones were replaced in the counterpoise and the rock slab moved softly upwards. Billy's heart was thumping as he peered out into velvet darkness. He drew back. '' Luck is with us," he whispered. " It has clouded up. Now, if only Copan can show us the way to this hiding-place, we can move the Dolphin without a soul being the wiser."

" I can find the way," replied Copan confidently, and all three slipped out into the Square. They waited and listened, but the only sound was the distant tinkle of a guitar, no doubt played by one of Castro's men.

Copan pointed to the side of the Square opposite to the temple. " That is our way," he said. Then between them the three set to wheeling the Dolphin across the open. A big machine like the Dolphin is heavy, and they had to go slowly, yet it was not long before Billy saw a blackness ahead and realised that they were approaching the ruined buildings bounding the north side of the Square.

" This way, señores," whispered Copan. " I do but hope that the wings are not too wide to pass through the entrance." The words were hardly out of his mouth before there came a loud shout from the centre of the Square, then a rifle squibbed off. " That's torn it," said Billy grimly. " Some of the beggars have found that the plane has gone."

CHAPTER SIXTEEN

A BAD BLUNDER

Cottle was coolest in a tight place. He looked back. "No need to get rattled, Billy," he answered quietly. "Those dagoes haven't a notion which way we've gone, and they don't seem to have any lights except old-fashioned lanterns. If we can get the plane into this hiding-place that Copan knows of the chances are all against their finding us."

"I expect you're right, sir," said Billy, pulling himself together. "Let's shove her along. But where is Copan?"

The little man had disappeared, and for the moment there was nothing to do but stand and wait. The row in the Square grew louder. There were at least a score of men running round the great monument, all gabbling and shouting at the top of their voices. It was lucky for Cottle and Billy that the night was so dark, for otherwise Castro's men must have seen the plane.

Copan came darting back. "I have found the place," he told them in a swift whisper. "This way, señores." The three got hold of the Dolphin again. Copan guided, and next moment they were in an opening between high walls. The left-hand wing banged against a wall on that side and they had to back the machine and try again.

" It's too narrow," gasped Billy. " She'll never go through."

" Tilt her a bit," ordered Cottle. " That's right. Yes, she will just go, but it's a tight fit. Where next, Copan?"

" Straight on, señor. Then turn to the right," Copan told them. The fat, rubber-shod wheels bumped over rough stone, then, acting on Copan's direction, they managed to swing her to the right, and Billy was suddenly conscious that they were under a roof of some sort. It was far too dark to see what it was, but it seemed to be quite close overhead.

" It is enough," said Copan. " Push her no farther, or perchance she will be wedged between roof and floor."

Billy swept the perspiration from his streaming forehead. " So far, so good," he said. " But see here, Professor, the Dolphin may be safe enough where she is for the rest of the night, but surely to goodness those sweeps are bound to find her in the morning."

" I was hoping you might have her ready to fly again by morning, Billy," said Cottle.

" I might be able to fix her up if I could use lights," Billy answered, " but that's the one thing one dare not do. Those dagoes must know that we can't have taken her far, and if they've got any sense at all they'll patrol the whole Square till morning."

" The question is whether they have as much sense as you credit them with, Billy. Now that Castro is in our hands I don't suppose they have

any leader worth talking about. My notion is
that they will very soon give up the search and
go back to their beds.''

'' I jolly well hope you are right,'' said Billy.
'' We'd best slip round and take a squint. We
can always bolt back if they're on the war-path.
Ask Copan to show us the way, for it's so dark
that I'm blessed if I know where to turn.''

Cottle spoke to the little man, and he agreed
that it would be best to see what was happening
in the Square and led the way out. Copan knew
every inch of the ground, and presently they were
all three standing close under the great wall and
peering out into the huge expanse of the Square.

'' They're still all round the monument,''
whispered Billy. '' What in the mischief are they
after?'' As he spoke he heard Copan, who was
close beside him, make a queer, gasping sound.
'' What's the matter?'' he demanded.

Copan answered, but though he spoke in
Spanish his words seemed to Billy to be all
jumbled together so that he could not make out
what the man said. But Cottle understood.
'' Don't you see, Billy?'' he said grimly. '' In
our anxiety to get the plane safe away we've forgotten the door. We never closed down the slab
and those beggars have found the opening.''

It was Billy's turn to gasp. Cottle turned to
Copan. '' Can they reach the cavern?'' he asked
quickly.

'' Of a certainty they will do so, señor,''
replied Copan hoarsely. '' They know that we

have come from there and they are mad for gold.''

Billy spoke. '' Then it's up to us to stop them,'' he said quietly. '' There are two machine-guns in the plane, Professor. If we get one out and give them a good peppering, we ought to be able to make a dash for it before they can realise what's up.''

Cottle hesitated. '' And if we fail we not only lose our lives but all those poor folk down below are butchered. Castro, also, is released, and so far as San Lucar is concerned there is the end of everything. Billy, it's not good enough.''

'' It's a big risk—I know that,'' said Billy, '' but it doesn't seem to me there's any choice.'' He broke off short. '' Hi, steady, Copan!'' he exclaimed as he caught the little man by the arm. Copan struggled violently. '' My wife, my children, they are at the mercy of those devils,'' he said thickly. Cottle laid a soothing hand on his shoulder. '' It will not help them if you are killed, chief,'' he said gently. '' And killed you will be for a certainty if you venture unarmed among those rascals. Listen one moment, for I think that I see a way of getting the better of our enemy.''

'' Speak,'' said Copan, '' but speak quickly, for even now those robbers are passing through the secret entrance.''

'' That door in the temple,'' said Cottle, '' the one through which you saved us during the fight this afternoon—is there any way of opening it from the outside?''

Copan's answer was instant. " Of a surety there is, but how can that help us, my lord, for the temple is in the hands of our enemies?"

" Our enemies are, most of them, out in the Square," Cottle answered. " I doubt if there are more than two or three in the temple itself. Chief, if you can lead us through the darkness to the temple chamber, Señor Hawkins and I will hold the outer door while you open the panel. Then, if we hasten, we can warn your people and meet the enemy on the narrow ledge. There, even without guns, we can surely defeat them."

"Thou art right," was Copan's quick reply. " Thy plan is better than mine. Come quickly."

" One moment," said Billy. " We must have weapons of some sort, and at present the only one we have is Castro's automatic. There are heavy spanners in the plane, and you can't get anything to beat 'em for close quarters."

" There are some bombs there too, if those beggars haven't stolen them," added Cottle. " We must use your lamp, Copan. Come with us."

Copan quickly led the way back to the plane. The light showed two things—first, that the plane was inside a low-roofed building where it was wonderfully hidden; secondly, that it had not been interfered with.

All his tools and stores were safe, and Billy took a couple of great spanners out of her tool chest, while Cottle filled his pockets with a number of his little bombs. Billy also grabbed a few slabs of chocolate, an electric torch with a spare battery, and a few other odds and ends. The whole business took but a few moments, then Copan shut up the lamp again and the three hurried out into the Square.

There were quite fifty men around the monument, and they were gabbling like monkeys. " Scared!" said Cottle briefly. " They suspect a trap of some kind."

" They'll find it," said Billy grimly.

Next moment the three were out in the open, running swiftly around the outer edges of the Square. They kept round the western side and, reaching the western end of the great temple, stopped a moment to look round.

" There are lights all through the blessed place," growled Billy.

" Yes," said Cottle, " but it doesn't follow that the men are there. I'm sure that most of them are out in the Square. At any rate, there doesn't seem to be any one on the porch. So our best plan will be to creep along quietly close under the wall until we reach the door of the big room. After that we shall have to take our chances."

" Right you are," replied Billy, and, taking a firmer grip on his spanner, went softly forward.

Luck was kind, and they reached the entrance to the room where they had met Castro without running into any of the rebels. But a strong light streamed from the entrance, and Cottle, who was leading, pulled up and signed to the others to keep still.

A voice came from somewhere inside. " *Diablo!*" it growled in coarse Spanish. " We waste our time here, Pedro. Let us go out into the plaza and see what is doing. If we stay where we are we miss our chance of treasure."

" Thou art a fool, Sanchez," retorted a second voice. " Were not the orders to remain on guard here?"

" Who cares for orders now that Castro is gone?" sneered the man called Sanchez. " With him away, one man is as good as another."

" So you may think," snapped back Pedro. " Yet well thou knowest that thou wouldst not dare say those words in the hearing of Juan Pecos. Short indeed would be thy shrift if thou didst."

" *Caramba!*" growled Sanchez. " Put me against Pecos and I would cut his heart from his body."

The other laughed. " And before thou didst draw thy knife Pecos would have filled thee with lead." Pedro's words seemed to discourage Sanchez, for he subsided into grumblings beneath his breath. Billy saw Cottle peer carefully around the great, carved door-post, take one swift glance within, then draw back. " Only two of them, so far as I can see," he whispered. " Billy, one is a big chap. Leave him to me. The other, Sanchez, is more your size. I think we can rush them before they realise what is up."

" Right," replied Billy eagerly.

" Remember, they must not shoot," warned Cottle urgently.

" Mine won't," grinned Billy. " Are you ready?"

" Not yet. I must explain to Copan." A word or two was enough for the quick-witted little chief. His jaw set firmly, and Billy as well as Cottle realised that he was going to be a very useful ally in a tight place.

Cottle took another glance around the door-post. " All right, Billy," he whispered briefly. " Get to it." As he spoke he leaped forward, and Billy, his big spanner tightly gripped in his right fist, shot after him. Both wore rubber-soled shoes, and Cottle was almost within striking distance of Pedro before the man heard him. Then he came round like a flash, but he was not as quick as Cottle. Before he could swing his rifle Cottle's left fist caught him under the jaw with the force of a pile-driver. The fellow's head clicked back and he went flat on his back, his rifle flying from his helpless hands and clattering across the floor.

Billy's man was a bit farther off than Cottle's, but Billy made up for the distance by the speed of his rush. The wretched Sanchez whirled to face his enemy, but before he realised what was happening the big wrench thudded on his ragged cap and he followed Pedro into oblivion.

" Good business!" cried Billy joyfully, and just then came a warning cry from Copan, and Billy barely had time to duck as a shot crashed out from the far corner, the bullet missing his head so narrowly that he felt the wind of it across his scalp. Unseen by any of them a third man had been resting on a straw mattress by the far wall, and now he was on his feet with his rifle to his shoulder.

He fired again, and Billy felt as if a red-hot iron had seared his left shoulder. In sheer desperation he hurled his wrench at the fellow. The man saw it coming and tried to duck, but Billy had thrown low and the heavy tool caught the rifleman in the stomach and doubled him up. Before he could recover Copan had reached him, and wresting his rifle from him gave him a crack over the head which stunned him.

" Are you hurt, Billy?" demanded Cottle.

" Nothing to shout about," Billy answered swiftly, " but those beggars in the Square must have heard. Copan, give me that rifle. I'll hold the entrance while you open the trap-door."

From Copan came a cry of dismay.

" What's the matter?" demanded Billy. It was Cottle who answered. " The door. It's open already. They've blown it in since we were here last." In the excitement of the last few moments none of them had had time to look round, but now Billy, glancing across at the wall, saw that a ragged hole yawned at the spot where they had passed through the hidden door.

" That's all right," he said sharply as he ran towards the opening. " So long as we can get to the second door ahead of this, I don't see that we are any the worse off."

" We shall have to be blamed quick about it," snapped Cottle. " Come on, Copan," he added.

" We must get through the second door before these fellows see where we are going."

" They are coming," gasped Copan as he made a dash through the opening. Cottle paused an instant before following and listened. " He's right!" he said to himself, for outside he heard the pounding of heavy brogans on the pavement of the Square. He snatched the nearest rifle and, scrambling quickly through the hole, flung himself down and waited.

" Professor, where are you?" came Billy's voice, echoing up the sloping gallery.

" Don't shout," hissed back Cottle. " When you've got the second door open, whistle."

" Right!" came back a hoarse whisper, and next moment the first of the rebels came panting into the temple chamber. He was a burly, bull-necked fellow, dirty and unshaven, and he pulled up in the entrance and stood staring round. Suddenly his eyes fell upon Sanchez, who lay flat on his back with arms outspread, and he gave a hoarse cry. *" Caramba!"* he yelled. " They have killed Sanchez."

" Who has killed him?" demanded a second, clattering in and peering over the shoulder of the first. Then he too saw Sanchez, and swore savagely at the sight. In a moment there were half a dozen more in the entrance, as rough a crowd as Cottle had ever set eyes upon. " This is getting a bit on the hot side," he said to himself with the ghost of a chuckle.

The bull-necked man was moving forward. In the dull light of an oil lantern which hung on the wall, Cottle saw the ugly red gleam in the fellow's eyes. " It is the cursed Inglese," the man said shrewdly.

" You talk foolishness, Ignacio," retorted another. " They got away in their flying machine."

Ignacio swung round on his companion. " It is you who are the fool, Felipè. The machine will not fly. Did not the general bring her down with that devil box of his? No, the Inglese came out of the hole under the Pointing Man, and they have gone down through the chamber here. Let us follow them quickly, for there is much treasure in the hidden caves beneath the city."

He stepped forward as he spoke and at that very moment Cottle heard Billy's whistle from the darkness beneath. He did not hesitate an instant, but taking one of his little smoke bombs from his pocket, flung it down. As the black smoke rose in a smothering cloud, he bolted down the passage. From behind came loud shouts, a rifle began to bark. Cottle bent his tall form nearly double, and kept as close as possible to the right-hand wall. Bullets came whistling past.

A gleam of blue light shone through the darkness and Cottle heard Billy's voice: " Here! The door is open. Give me your hand."

" Take my rifle," panted Cottle, and, as Billy seized it, he flung himself through the narrow opening into the side passage.

CHAPTER SEVENTEEN

CUT OFF

BILLY and Copan flung themselves at the door. It was a great slab of rock which ran in grooves and worked, not by a lever, but by a double-purchase pulley. "It's stuck," gasped Billy in a horror-stricken tone, and almost as he spoke a man burst through the coiling smoke in the passage outside. It was the bull-necked Ignacio, and as he saw the opening in the wall he gave a shout of triumph. It was the last sound he ever made, for Cottle, snatching up the rifle, shot him dead.

Then he flung all his weigh on the raw-hide rope, and the great slab came creaking downwards. "I had to do it," he said as, panting with their exertions, the three stood together in the glow of Copan's lamp.

"If you hadn't it meant finish for all of us," Billy answered. "I only hope that none of the others saw the slab drop."

"There were no others in sight," said Cottle. "We are safe enough at this end. It's the ledge from which the attack will come, so the sooner we are there to meet it, the better."

Without another word they were off down the cross passage, and within a very few moments reached the big cave. There all was quiet and Copan's face showed how intense was his relief.

" Thanks be to the gods, we are in time," he said, then gave a curious, whistling call and instantly a score of his men came running up from every direction, each drawing his sword as he came.

Copan spoke to them in their own language, a few brief sentences, and at once they all turned and ran towards the far side of the cave.

" Plucky as they make them," said Cottle to Billy. " There's fine fighting stuff in those little chaps."

" They're all right," agreed Billy heartily as he and Cottle followed Copan; " but what good are those little swords of theirs against rifles? I wish to goodness we had one of the machine-guns out of the plane."

" It certainly would be useful," replied Cottle. At any rate, we have a rifle and a couple of pistols, and I, for one, should not care to tackle the ledge with even one armed man to hold it. The great thing is that we are in time," Cottle said, as he and Billy reached the outer entrance, and found themselves facing the gorge.

By this time the sky had cleared, and although the moon was not yet up, the great tropical stars sent a dim light into the depths of the vast abyss.

Copan turned to them. " It is well, señores," he said happily. " Our enemies have not yet reached the ledge."

Billy caught him by the arm. " I'm not so sure about that. Tell your men to keep quiet, and listen!"

Copan whispered an order, and in the silence

that followed, a slight shuffling sound was heard coming from far up the ledge. " I told you so," whispered Billy. " Here they are."

" Luckily, very slowly," said Cottle. " I don't suppose they like the ledge any better than we did."

Copan spoke: " There are many of them, señores, and they have the fire tubes. Nor is there any way of closing this entrance, for, as you see, it is wide and there is no door."

" You mean that they may rush us," said Cottle. It seems to me that the only thing to do is to destroy the path."

" But there is no time for that, lord," Copan answered. " Even should all our men work together it would be morning before they could break a gap great enough to stop these thieves."

" Trouble not yourself, chief," Cottle said comfortingly. " Señor Hawkins and I have means whereby we can burst these rocks in an instant of time. But if we do so, do not we also cut off from ourselves and from you any way of escape from these caverns?"

" That is true, señor. Yet a gap can be bridged if it be not too wide, and better is it to take the risk of being cut off rather than that these robbers shall destroy us all."

" Then I have your leave?" said Cottle swiftly. " Billy, you have the dynamite, and I think one stick will just do the trick. But you will have to be quick, for if those fellows once suspect what is up and start shooting it's not going to be healthy for any one of us who is on the ledge."

"No, by jove, it isn't," agreed Billy; "but luckily it's far too dark for them to see what we are up to. Here's the dynamite. Keep the light off the ledge until I've got the thing ready." He stepped back under the rock arch and set to preparing his dynamite.

Cottle stood outside listening. Presently he spoke again. "Be quick, Billy. They're coming now, and, by the sound, there are a lot of them."

"Right!" said Billy. "It's ready now. But where's the best place to use it?"

Cottle spoke to Copan, and the little chief understood at once. "Ten paces upwards from the doorway," he told them. "With my lord's leave, I myself will place the fire stick."

"It is not exactly a fire stick, and one of us must handle it," said Cottle swiftly. "Give it to me, Billy; I insist."

He took the primed stick from Billy and strode swiftly up the ledge, counting his steps as he went. From the darkness above came the shuffling steps of many men, and suddenly round the curve of the great cliff a light shone out as the leader came into sight carrying a lantern.

Billy stood at the doorway, the rifle ready in his hand. He was quivering with excitement, for he knew what Copan and the others did not know—that Cottle would have to light a match and so make himself a target for the rebels. Next moment came the scratch of the match and there was Cottle, cool as a cucumber, touching the match to the fuse of the dynamite stick. Instantly from above came a shout, and on top of the shout a shot. The bullet must have passed directly over Cottle's head for Billy heard it strike the cliff side close above him. But Cottle had already wheeled round, and bent double, was rushing back to shelter. Two more shots followed him, but these were wild, and the next instant Billy had the Professor by the arm and had swung him into safety under the arch. Crack! Crack! came two sharp reports from above. "They've spotted the dynamite; they are shooting at it," gasped Billy. "If they hit it we are done."

"They haven't got it yet," said Cottle, and his words were drowned by a shattering explosion. For an instant both sides of the gorge leaped into vivid light, while the whole cliff trembled with the back blast of the explosion. The roar was followed by a thudding, rushing sound as a great mass of rock went thundering down into the abyss.

Cottle turned to Copan. "We are safe," he said.

Copan nodded. "Truly it was like the lightning bolt," he answered gravely. "Yes, lord, thou hast saved us from these wicked ones. Would that thou couldst also save us from the second danger."

"What's that?" demanded Cottle. "Do you mean these Indians?"

Copan shook his head. "It is not of the Indians I speak, but of hunger. Our food is nearly at an end, and now, as thou dost see, we can no longer reach our fields or gardens."

For once Cottle looked a little dismayed. "Short of food!" he repeated. "That is serious. But explain, chief. Where are your gardens? Where do you grow your corn and vegetables?"

"Within the city, lord," replied Copan. "In the old days the whole plain was fields and gardens, but for many years past there have been but few of us, and, because of the Araks, we have not dared to venture far from our strongholds. So we have used the waste spaces within the city and they have sufficed to produce food for my people."

"I understand," said Cottle; "but I take it, then, that you have not been able to cultivate your ground since Castro invaded Sanat?"

"Not by day, lord, but by night we have been able to visit our gardens, going out by the cliff path which leads to a secret way. Now, however, thou seest that the path can no longer be used."

"But the gap can be bridged," replied Cottle.

"True, lord, but now that those thieves have learned of the path they will guard it and will fall upon us should we venture upon it."

Cottle nodded. "You are right, chief. And I will admit that we are in a tight place. But surely you have a reserve store, for even before Castro came you lived in danger of invasion from these Araks?"

"Again thou are right, lord," replied Copan. "By my orders, grain for a month's supply was hoarded in a chamber of the great temple. But when I sent men to fetch food from this chamber

they found that the thieving Spaniards had discovered our store and stolen all.''

'' Stolen it!'' cried Billy who had been listening eagerly. '' The brutes! But I say, Professor, can't we get back on them, somehow?''

'' We will try it if it is any way possible,''
declared Cottle. '' Tell me, chief, have you any
idea where Castro's men keep their stores?''

'' In some part of the great temple,'' Copan
answered. '' It is in my mind that they fear to
go far abroad.''

'' Why?'' questioned Cottle.

'' They fear the angry ghosts of the old
people,'' replied Copan. '' Also, there are many
serpents in the ruins.''

'' Snakes, eh?'' said Billy speaking in English.
'' That's enough, I guess, without the ghosts.''

'' You are wrong, Billy,'' said Cottle gravely.
'' These rebels are riddled with superstition; that
I know well. I dare say they are afraid of the
snakes, but I am certain they are much more
terrified of the ghosts.''

A slow smile dawned on Billy's face. '' Then
why not work on their superstition, Professor?
Couldn't we dress ourselves up as ghosts, and
walk in on them in the middle of the night? We
should put the wind up them properly.''

Cottle nodded. '' It's not a bad idea, Billy.
The trouble is, first, we don't know where the
fellows keep their stores, and secondly that, as
Copan says, they are sure to guard the cliff path,
while as for the other way, we simply dare not
use it again.''

Billy was not dismayed. " But the whole place is riddled with tunnels and secret passages. Surely Copan can put us on to some other way up topside. Ask him, Professor."

Copan's intelligent face lit up as he listened to Cottle, and he answered in such rapid Spanish that Billy could not follow what he said. Cottle explained. " He thinks the plan might work, and he does know of another way out. But he says it is too difficult to carry stores along it. I gather it means a bit of real rock climbing. Yet if we once get the stuff we might bring it out by one of our regular ways, for I still have a smoke bomb or two. The crab is this, that none of us knows in what part of the temple they keep their stores, and we certainly shan't have time to go messing about searching. The whole essence of the business will be surprise."

" Oh, we can get at that information all right," said Billy quietly.

Cottle looked at him. " How?" he demanded curtly.

Billy grinned. " Castro knows," he answered.

Cottle gave a short, sharp laugh. " I never thought of that, Billy." Then he turned suddenly serious. " But he's hardly likely to tell," he added.

" Not at first, perhaps," said Billy; " but after a day or two's starvation I shouldn't wonder if he changed his mind."

Cottle nodded. " You're an ingenious young fiend, Billy. Still, I dare say you are right. Very well then, I will explain matters to Copan, and after that we'd best get some sleep. It's been a fairly strenuous day, and, on the whole, I think we have not done so badly. At any rate, we have found where the green gold comes from and we have collared Castro."

" But we have lost the plane," returned Billy with sudden bitterness.

Cottle laid a kindly hand on Billy's shoulder. " I don't agree with you, Billy. I believe the machine is safe where she is. And perhaps I have more reason for saying so than you imagine."

" What do you mean?" cried Billy eagerly. But Cottle would not tell.

" Wait till to-morrow," was all he would say. " Now we must get some rest. And your arm—, that's got to be looked to."

" My arm. I'd forgotten all about it in the excitement," confessed Billy. " Don't bother about it. It's only a scratch."

" You'll let me be judge of that," said Cottle firmly. " Come along." They went through the great, pillared hall to their sleeping apartment with its blue light and its clear bathing pool, and Billy stripped off his coat and shirt. His shirt was stuck to his arm and he winced a bit as Cottle sponged it loose and examined the wound. " Yes, you got off cheaply, Billy," he said. " All the same, it's a nasty place, and would precious soon poison if not looked to." He took a little carved box from his pocket. " This is some stuff of Copan's which he says will cure any wound. Care to try it?"

"Smells simply topping," said Billy. "Yes, put some on."

Cottle did so and the result simply amazed Billy. "Why it takes away the pain like magic!" he exclaimed. "I say, Professor, if ever we get home again we could make a fortune out of this stuff."

"Perhaps we shall take a fortune home, anyhow," smiled Cottle as he tied up the arm. "Now get right to bed. I don't suppose we shall get much sleep to-morrow night."

Billy obeyed orders, and inside ten minutes was sound asleep. Cottle watched him a few moments, but instead of following his example, slipped silently out into the main cave where Copan awaited him.

"You wish to see the rebel dog?" said Copan.

"Yes, I want to have a few words with the gentleman," agreed Cottle. "But tell me, chief, how is it you speak such excellent Spanish? You must have been away from Sanat at some time or another?"

"No, lord, I have lived here with my people all my life. It was my father taught me. Since the days of the invaders the chief of the Chiapas has always learned their language, for there has been a prophecy that one day they would reach our hidden city and then knowledge of their language would be necessary."

"And now the prophecy has come true," said Cottle gravely.

"It is so," replied Copan. "Yet with your help, lord, we shall drive out these evil ones."

"We will do our best," Cottle told him. "And once that is done, I promise you that Sanat shall never again be disturbed by outsiders without your permission."

Copan straightened his small self and his usually solemn face softened. "Thou art a man, lord. Verily I believe that thy coming will be our salvation."

He walked forward and Cottle followed.

CHAPTER EIGHTEEN

CASTRO OWNS UP

COTTLE had not yet seen Castro's prison. He found it to be a low-roofed vault, shut off from the main cave by a door of solid bronze. The place was lit by one of the ever-burning blue lights, and the air was quite fresh. There was a bed, similar to those in the room reserved for Cottle and Billy, and a table and chair.

Castro was lying on the bed but he was not asleep. He sat up as Cottle and Copan came in. "You are, perhaps, bringing me some supper?" he said softly.

"That is exactly what I have come to talk to you about, Señor Castro," replied Cottle. "I fear there is little supper for any of us. Your cut-throats have stolen all the available food, and the object of my visit is to ask you what they have done with it."

Castro did not answer at first. He sat staring at Cottle, seemingly trying to make out whether he was serious or not. Then an ugly grin twisted the corners of his thin lips. "So already you begin to find how foolish you have been to oppose me, Señor Cottle," he remarked.

Cottle looked at him composedly. "Well, I don't know. To capture the rebel leader, and lay out a dozen or so of his best men is not so bad for a first day's work."

Castro made a scornful gesture. "You have me; I acknowledge that. But what good will it do you? Without food or your aeroplane, you are perfectly helpless. And even if you have killed a dozen of my men, what is it when I have hundreds?"

"Oh, the plane is quite safe, señor," Cottle answered. "We took it out of the Square this evening."

Castro roused at last. "You lie," he spat out.

"Your manners leave something to be desired, Señor Castro," Cottle remarked. "Still, one can hardly blame you for feeling peevish, especially since I know the value which you set upon the Dolphin. But to return to what we were speaking of, where is the food stored?"

Castro's stiff black hair seemed to bristle with rage. "Go to blazes and find out!" he snarled.

"I don't know about going to blazes, but I shall certainly find out," said Cottle. "*Buenos noches, señor*. I trust that hunger will not interfere with your sleep." And, leaving Castro boiling, he left the prison cave.

" The evil one will not speak?" questioned Copan quietly.

Cottle smiled. " He is angry to-night," he answered. " To-morrow I think that he will perhaps be more ready to talk."

" It may be so, lord," agreed the little man. " Now it would be well that thou shouldst sleep."

" The guard—is it set?" asked Cottle.

" It is set," was the answer.

Cottle nodded. It was proof of how entirely he trusted the chief that he went straight to bed and was soon sleeping as peacefully as Billy.

It was the sound of splashing that roused him. Billy's bed was empty, and Billy himself had just taken a header into the deep clear pool. He came up and dashed the water from his eyes. " Seven o'clock, sir," he said. " All quiet in Sanat, and the women are cooking breakfast."

" Going to be a slim meal, I'm afraid," replied Cottle as he flung off his clothes and went head foremost into the pool. " How's the arm, Billy?" continued Cottle as he rose to the surface.

" Good as ever. No pain, no inflammation. I tell you, that stuff of Copan's is better than anything you could buy in a chemist's shop."

" Yes, they do know things—these old people," agreed Cottle as he climbed out and picked up a towel.

They had just finished dressing when Copan, himself, came to summon them to breakfast. It was a very simple meal—just mush, that is, a porridge made of ground maize.

Afterwards, Copan took them through his underground home. All round the main cave were other smaller rock chambers, some used as sleeping-rooms, others as workshops. In one was a very cleverly designed forge where the bronze implements were made of metal quarried in the valley; in another, women were at work, weaving cloth from native cotton; a third was a shoe-maker's shop where sandals were made with thickly plaited soles. In a small room an old man mixing medicines from herbs, who smiled gravely when Billy explained how much good the oint-ment had done him.

But the most interesting to Cottle was the chamber in which the lights were made and looked after. He turned to Copan, asking eager questions.

But here, of course, there was trouble, for Copan had no Spanish to explain the scientific side of the business, and Cottle, unfortunately, could not understand the Chiapa language. Still, he did gather this much—that the lamps were made out of crystals treated with radium emana-tions so that they gave a perfectly cold light which lasted an immense time. In this chemical depart-ment there were other things of interest to Billy and Cottle. A metal tank in one corner was filled with a liquid substance which looked like blue flame, but which, as Copan assured them, was perfectly harmless. Here, again, the Professor was wild to find of what it was made, but, as before, Copan had no words to explain.

Billy, however, had no doubts. " Ghost

stuff!" he cried joyfully. "I say, Professor, what price a rig dipped in this?"

"It would certainly look pretty ghastly," agreed Cottle. "I will ask Copan if we can use it."

Copan explained that in the old days this blue fire was used for painting signs that could be read at night. He added that Billy was welcome to try it on the rebels.

Billy set to work at once and got one of the women to make him a kind of robe in shape rather like a nightshirt.

Later in the day, Cottle went to see Castro again. He came back frowning slightly and looking very thoughtful, and Billy, knowing better than to ask questions, waited for him to speak. Cottle walked across the cave, through the passage, and out on to the ledge facing the ravine.

Cottle stood silent a moment, gazing down into the darksome depths of the giant cleft, then suddenly turned to Billy. "The odd thing is that he was not lying," he said abruptly.

"Castro, you mean?" replied the quick-witted Billy.

"Castro, of course. He has told me where the food is stored."

"Ah, I thought he'd crumble after a day without grub," said Billy with satisfaction. "Then to-night we'll raid the place, and to-morrow these poor people will get a square meal."

"I hope so," said Cottle, but he looked so gloomy that Billy was puzzled.

" What's the matter, sir?" he asked outright.

" I wish I knew, Billy."

" But you always know," insisted Billy.
" That's the beauty of it, and you said that
Castro was speaking the truth."

" The truth, but not all the truth," said Cottle.
" And it is beyond me to read what the fellow
was keeping from me."

Billy looked up quickly. " You think then
that there is some catch about it?"

" I am sure of it," said the other gravely. Yet
whatever the risk, we must take it. We start at
nine o'clock."

Copan had told them that the only way to the
upper ground was a stiff one, and Billy found
that this was, if anything, less than the truth.
Once out on the ledge, they turned left instead of
right and made their way down a slight slope for
some little distance. Then Copan, who was leading, stopped and Billy saw that there was a cleft
to the left, cutting into the cliff at right-angles to
the ledge. " This is our road," whispered Copan,
and turned into the cleft.

It was very narrow and dark, and presently
Billy found himself scrambling up a sort of
giants' staircase. It would have been a nasty
climb in broad daylight; under the uncertain
glimmer of the stars it was abominably dangerous.

Half-way up Billy found himself close to
Cottle. " How are we going to get the stores
back down here?" he panted.

" Don't worry. These chaps will do it all

right," replied Cottle. " They climb like cats."
He was right. Copan's men, a dozen in number,
went up over the piled crags in a perfectly
marvellous way. All were armed with swords
and also with cross-bows. They carried ropes
and lanterns, but the latter were kept closed.
Copan had warned them against making any
sound.

When at last they reached the top Billy drew
a long breath of relief, and looked round. He
found that they were on fairly level ground,
which was littered with the ruins of fallen buildings. A little beyond he could see several of the
curious beehive-shaped houses, and farther away
the great mass of the temple rose against the star-
strewn sky. A few lights showed in the temple,
but there was no other sign of life.

" Walk carefully," whispered Copan. " There
are many snakes among the ruins."

" Sounds cheerful," muttered Billy. " Which
way do we go, Professor?"

" The storehouse is close to the temple,"
replied Cottle. " There is a large bush just
behind it. I think I shall recognise it without
trouble."

" What price my ghost dress? Do I put it on
now?" asked Billy.

" Not yet, and don't talk more than you have
to."

Billy subsided, and for the next few minutes
had his work cut out to pick his way by the faint
starlight among the masses of broken masonry.
Then Copan and Cottle stopped, and the latter

pointed to a dense mass of bush beyond which rose the dome-shaped top of one of the ancient houses. "That's the place," whispered Cottle.

The building was one of the usual beehive shape, but bigger than the others. It was, however, too dark to see more than that. As a rule, Cottle never wasted a moment when there was anything to be done, but now he hesitated in a very unusual way. "There'll be a guard over the place," suggested Billy. "Perhaps Castro thought we shouldn't think of that and was hoping they would mop us up."

"No," replied Cottle slowly. "That is too obvious, Billy. It was something quite different from that the fellow had in his mind. Hang it all!" he said with sudden irritation. "I wish I knew what it was."

Billy was troubled. "Let me go forward and have a look," he begged. "I'll come back at once if I see anything suspicious."

Cottle cut him short. "No. This is my show. You stick where you are, Billy." At this moment Copan, who had gone on a little, came slipping silently back out of the gloom. "There are no guards, lord," he said softly to Cottle. "One of my men has been all around the building. What sayest thou? Was the rebel leader lying?"

"No, chief, what he told me was true, and it is in this building that the grain is stored. But it is in my mind that he was keeping something back."

"If it is in thy mind, it is true," said Copan

193

simply. " It may be that there is an ambush laid by these thieves."

Cottle shook his head. " That is not likely, chief, for Castro cannot have sent word to lay such an ambush. Inquire of thy man if there is an opening into the building."

" That he has told me already," replied Copan. " There is a door on the side facing the temple. It is of stone, and hidden like the doors of all the old houses."

" Can we open it?" asked Cottle.

" Yes, lord," Copan answered him, " for all doors in the city are made alike."

Cottle turned to Billy. " Keep watch, Billy," he ordered. " Copan will open the door for me, and I shall go in."

" I wish you'd let me come with you, sir," begged Billy, but Cottle cut him short. " You will obey orders," he said with unusual sternness. " If there is any alarm, do not fire. Let your men use their cross-bows if they like, but above all things there must be no noise."

As he and Copan went softly forward Billy advanced a little so as to be within sight of the front of the building. The Chiapas, who had evidently had their orders from Copan, spread out a little, then took cover behind blocks of broken masonry.

Billy's heart beat uncomfortably as he watched Cottle and Copan approach the building. He was not easy. He felt that danger threatened, and the darkness and the oppressive silence and heat of the night added to his discomfort. There was light enough to see Copan feeling with both hands upon the wall, evidently for the spring or lever which worked the door. He found it, and with a slight grating sound the stone moved up leaving a black oblong opening in the stone wall of the building.

Then Billy saw Cottle's tall form pass Copan and move on into the inner darkness of the doorway. Half-unconsciously Billy took a step forward, and as he did so there was a fresh grating sound followed by a heavy thud, and to his dismay he saw that the door had fallen back into its place, imprisoning Cottle within the dark interior of the building.

Forgetting everything else, Billy sprang forward to Copan's side. " The door, why did it close?" he asked.

" I know not," replied Copan, and for the first time since he had met the little man Billy realised that the Chiapa chief was frightened.

" Open it," hissed Billy. " Where is the spring?"

Copan was already feeling for it, and presently Billy saw him press with all his force on a certain stone.

Nothing happened. There was no sign of the door moving. " You are pressing on the wrong place," said Billy hoarsely.

" Alas, no," was the answer. " It is the right stone, but there is trickery. The door has fallen and we cannot move it. The white lord is imprisoned within, and there is no way of releasing him."

CHAPTER NINETEEN

BLUE BLAZES

" THERE must be some way of getting him out," snapped Billy as he stared at the closed door. He paused a moment. " Yes, of course there is," he said with sudden relief, for he remembered how, when flying above the city, he had looked down and seen the open tops of these oddly shaped dwellings. " We can get him out, all right. Give me a rope."

In his excitement he spoke in English, then, seeing Copan's blank look, repeated his words in Spanish. A moment later one of the Chiapas handed him a coil of strong rope spun from some vegetable fibre, and Billy, snatching it, picked up a stone and quickly fastened it to one end of the cord. Then, swinging the loose end round his head, he cast it clear over the top of the building so that the stone fell upon the far side.

" Catch hold of it," ordered Billy, but the quick-witted little man had already seen what Billy was after, and two of them, seizing the loose end, held it tight.

" I'm going up," Billy told Copan, and, catching hold of the rope, set to scrambling up the wall. The masonry, formerly quite smooth and solid, had been loosened by many centuries of weather, to say nothing of earthquakes, and Billy found no great difficulty in clambering up the sloping wall. But when he reached the top he got a nasty shock, for the central opening had been roofed in. Rough timbers had been laid across and thatched with palm leaves.

Billy drew a knife and set to carving the thatch, and to his great relief found that he could get through it. He ripped and tore at the stuff until he had managed to make a hole, and to his great joy at once saw a gleam of light beneath.

" That you, Billy?" came Cottle's familiar voice.

" Yes, you're not hurt, are you?"

" I'm all right. Send me down a rope. You have a guard posted?"

" Yes, Copan's men are looking out." As he spoke, Billy pulled up the loose end of the rope and dropped it down inside. " Are you coming up, sir?" he asked in a swift whisper.

" Not yet. I must send up some grain first. It's the one thing we can't go back without."

" Be quick then," breathed Billy.

There was a short pause, then Cottle's voice calling to him to haul up. Billy braced himself and hauled. It was all he could do to get the sack up to the top, but he managed it, and called to Copan that he was lowering it down the outside of the wall. It had hardly reached the ground before there came the hoot of the little night owl, and Billy knew it for the alarm signal.

" They're coming," he whispered down to Cottle. " Come up, sir, quick as you can."

" Leave me the rope," Cottle answered quite calmly. " I can find my way up. And as for you, get down quickly, Billy, and try your ghost outfit. If it works it will give us breathing space. If it doesn't we are no worse off than we are now."

Billy realised at once that Cottle was right, and went down the rope like a lamp-lighter.

Copan was waiting anxiously. "Señor, what can we do?" he asked. "My men say that a strong party of Castro's thieves approaches."

"My ghost dress," Billy answered swiftly as he picked up the little bundle which contained it. "Help me on with it."

"You are right. I had forgotten," whispered back Copan, "but keep out of sight until you have it on."

One of Copan's men darted up. "Shall we shoot?" he asked rapidly, but Billy ordered him to wait. "If they run," he said to Copan, "then let them go. If not, let your men use their bows. But no noise if you can help it. We are too close to their barracks in the temple."

Without waiting for any reply he wrapped a black robe about himself, completely hiding his flaming ghost dress, and, bending double, ducked away among the ruins which littered the ground. Moving softly as possible he presently caught the sound of footsteps. At once he pulled up under shelter of a mass of fallen masonry and stood, stock still, peering out into the gloom and listening intently.

"A dozen or more," he said to himself. "I'd jolly well like to know how they got to know there was any one about. Looks to me as if the fall of

the door must have warned them in some way.
No doubt that's what the dear Castro had in
mind.''

His reflections were cut short by the sudden
appearance of several shadowy figures. They
were marching straight towards the storehouse
and would pass, he saw, within a few yards of
where he was standing. '' Wonder if they'll
scare or shoot,'' was the thought that flashed
through his mind as he dropped the black robe
and suddenly stepped out into the open.

If Billy could have seen himself in a looking-
glass he would not have had much doubt. Billy's
robe threw out lambent flames, great tongues of
blue fire which flickered and leapt like those of
burning brandy. And the robe had a hood which
also flamed in the same way while leaving his
face a mere dark gap.

The moment he stepped out into the open he
was conscious of a sudden stop on the part of the
rebels. He paused an instant, then suddenly
raised his burning arms high above his head and
walked straight towards the enemy.

It was a plucky thing to do, for badly
frightened men will frequently go crazy, and,
instead of running, attack the object that scares
them. But Billy's appearance was ghastly enough
to have scared a regiment of white men, and as
for these superstitious dagoes, not one of them
had the slightest doubt but that this was one of
the spirits which they firmly believed haunted
the ruins. With shrieks of terror the whole party
turned and ran.

By the sounds they were flinging down their rifles, and a heavy thud and a cry of pain told him that at least one had come a cropper. Anxious to make the most of the scare, Billy walked rapidly after the fugitives. Next moment he stumbled over a rifle and nearly fell, so he stopped and waited a moment to see what was happening. There was no need to worry, for the rebels were running for their lives, and already the sound of their flying footsteps was dying away in the direction of the temple. Ducking down behind a big stone, Billy pulled off his ghost robe, then picked up the rifle and hurried back to the storehouse. " It's all right," he told Copan. " They ran for their lives. Where is Señor Cottle?"

" He is still within the storehouse," Copan told him.

" Very good. Then I will go up again," said Billy, and without a moment's delay went scrambling up the rope again. " It's all right, sir," he told Cottle. " The beggars ran like rabbits. By this time they are all back in the temple."

" They'll be out again," Cottle prophesied. " Still, it gives us a breathing space, and we must use it. Here is another sack. Haul away."

They worked like fury and soon had out a dozen sacks of grain. Then to Billy's horror there came again the low hoot of the owl. " They're coming," he whispered down to Cottle.

" Then they have someone to lead them,"

replied Cottle in a tone of certainty. " All right, Billy, I'll come up." A few moments later both were on the ground again beside Copan. " See here, chief," said Cottle calmly, " the first thing is to get the grain back to the cave. Can your men carry it?"

" They can, lord, but it will require two to each sack, and it leaves none to hold the way against these Spanish thieves."

" Do not worry about that," Cottle told him. " The Señor Hawkins and I will hold the path."

" They will kill you," Copan exclaimed.

" We take a good deal of killing," smiled back Cottle. " Now go, I beg of you, and get the grain back to the cave. Later we will follow you."

When Cottle spoke like that there was no question of disobedience, and Copan turned reluctantly away and set his men to gathering up the bags and carrying them off. Cottle turned to Billy. " Wish I knew who was leading this new crowd," he whispered. " A lot depends on that."

" Go forward. Straight to the storehouse," came a voice out of the gloom. It was harsh, high-pitched, and Billy recognised it instantly. " Pecos," he whispered in Cottle's ear. " It's that little reptile Pecos."

" I thought as much," answered Cottle in an equally low voice. " Then it's us for trouble, Billy. Step back a bit—behind the storehouse. They will be delayed for a little while they search the place, and just now every second counts. That's a nasty place for Copan to get the grain down, and he needs all of ten minutes law."

The two slipped back behind the storehouse, and, as they took cover under a pile of crumbling masonry, Pecos' sharp voice rang out again. "What are you waiting for? Get on, you white-livered cowards."

Billy grinned. "They haven't got over the ghost yet," he whispered.

"Here. Give a light," snarled Pecos, and on the other side of the storehouse shone the gleam of a torch. "Ah, it is as I thought," he continued. "Someone has been at the door. Well, whoever he is, we have him safely. Here, Jose, stand by with your rifle while I open." Billy listened eagerly, and next moment came the familiar grating sound of the great slab sliding back. "The light, Jose!" came Pecos' voice. "Shine the light inside, fool!"

"There's no one there, Captain," came Jose's voice in a tone of surprise.

"Don't talk nonsense," snapped back Pecos. "Of course he is there. He is hiding. Keep your rifle to your shoulder and be ready to shoot."

Silence a moment, then Pecos spoke again. "Come out of it, Englishman. Come out, you are covered."

Billy gurgled with joy. "Dear old Pecos is going to get a nasty jar," he whispered to Cottle, but Cottle nudged him sharply.

"Shut up, Billy," he muttered.

"There is no one here, Captain," came Jose's voice again. "And look, there is a hole in the roof."

Pecos exploded in a volley of oaths. "It is

your fault, fools," he ended. " If you had the courage of mice you would have caught these thieves instead of running back with silly stories of a ghost."

" But it was a ghost, Captain," remonstrated one of the men. " We all saw it and the blue flames which dripped from it. It was a Spirit of Death."

" Spirit of your grandmother!" sneered Pecos. " Get out of this, and let me see which way those thieves went."

The light showed round the side of the building, and Cottle touched Billy's arm. " Here's where the trouble starts," he said. " Be careful now, Billy. We have to hold them off for at least another five minutes in order to give Copan a chance to get his grain away."

" What about letting 'em have it, then?" said Billy. " We've two rifles and a pistol. A volley when they weren't expecting it would knock 'em silly."

" No," whispered Cottle. " No shooting unless we have to. And keep out of sight, for here they are."

As he spoke Pecos himself came into sight, and by the light of a lantern carried by one of his men Billy easily recognised his sallow face.

Pecos was examining the ground. " It was those miserable Chiapas," he snapped out. " Yes, here are their tracks. A number of them, too. But, of course, they were led by the cursed Inglese." He turned upon his men in a passion of rage. " These were your ghosts, you miserable cowards. And you have let them go off with at least a dozen sacks of grain." He paused and again examined the footprints. " But they cannot have gone far," he added. " If we are quick we shall catch them before they reach their underground haunts. Listen to me, men. If you stop them I shall say no more about your cowardice, and if you catch either of the Inglese the man who does so shall have a hundred dollars reward."

" We will catch them for you, Captain," declared Jose, who was a great bull of a fellow. " We will catch them. They cannot have gone fast, carrying those loads." As he spoke he pushed past Pecos and the others followed.

Billy saw Cottle raise his rifle above the pile of ruined masonry which sheltered them. " I hate to be the one to start shooting," he whispered, " but there's no help for it. We must stop them. I will fire the first shot at the lantern, and if that stops them, well and good. If not—it's on their own heads." Billy saw him take quick aim and pull the trigger. With the report of his rifle came the crackle of splintering glass, and a yell of dismay from Jose as the lantern was smashed to a thousand pieces.

" The Inglese!" cried one of the men in a tone of terror.

Pecos' voice was sharp and angry. " Fools, there are but two of them, and you are twenty. Are you cowards as well as fools?" Billy heard a hoarse growl. Then by the faint starlight he saw the whole body charging forward.

Next instant Cottle's rifle spat death, and Billy too began to fire. In spite of the bad light the distance was so short that hardly a bullet failed to reach its target. Some, indeed, of the nickel-tipped missiles drove through two bodies at once. Yells and screams filled the air, and it seemed to Billy that quite half the attacking force dropped before the trigger of his rifle clicked and he realised he had fired every cartridge in the magazine. The rest of the rebels vanished, springing away to one side or the other and crouching down behind any sort of cover.

" That's stopped 'em for the moment," whispered Cottle. " But load up, Billy."

" I've no more cartridges, sir. This is the rifle I picked up. It's an old-fashioned .44 bore, and I'm afraid yours won't fit."

" Then take my pistol," said Cottle swiftly, " and follow me. We must retreat, and that's the worst part of a fight like this." Bent double, he crawled away, and Billy, dropping his useless rifle, followed. The ruins, which lay everywhere, gave good cover, but at the same time made the going desperately difficult. The pair had not gone fifty yards before they heard Pecos' voice shouting to his men. " Jose, Almagro, where are you? Forward, follow them. Spread out and surround them. Get between them and the ravine. A thousand dollars to him who kills or captures them!"

Cottle paused a moment for Billy to come alongside. " So we failed to finish Master Pecos," he said grimly. " That spells trouble,

Billy, for if they do get between us and the ravine we are done."

" They don't know our way down," replied Billy. " Come on, sir. Let's make a run for it."

" No. That would be madness. They would hear us, perhaps see us. We must creep and crawl. That is our only chance." Still bending almost double, he dodged away, taking cover as cleverly as a Red Indian, and Billy followed. Billy's ears were straining for any sound which might betray the approach of an enemy, and presently he caught the rattle of a loose stone away to the left. " There's one of them," he whispered, but Cottle, who was some little distance away, did not hear.

Billy hurried after him. All of a sudden he saw a dark form rise from behind a bush close on Cottle's right and caught a gleam of steel blue in the starlight. Springing upright, he thrust forward his pistol and pulled the trigger.

With the flare of the explosion the rebel went over backwards with a crash. At the same instant two other men leapt out from a bush to the right and one fired at Billy, but in the hurry missed him. The other hurled himself upon Cottle. The two went down together. Then before Billy could fire again something crashed upon his head from behind and down he too fell on his face on the hard ground.

CHAPTER TWENTY

THE GUARDED WAY

BILLY came to himself with a faint light shining in his eyes, but he was so dazed that it was some moments before he realised that it was the moon. He tried to move, but the attempt sent such a throb of pain through his head that he dropped back and lay still. He found himself lying on his back on hard ground close under a low, thick bush. The moon had just risen above the valley cliffs to the east, and its slanting rays struck his face and silvered the ruins which surrounded him. Everything was deathly still.

Billy's head was one ache, and when he put his hand up to it he found his hair matted with dried blood. Memory came back to him, and he remembered how he had shot the man who was trying to stab Cottle, and how he had been floored by a blow from behind.

But how was it that he had been left there? A pang of terror struck cold to his heart, for it came to him that Cottle must be dead. If he had come through the fight, alive, his first thought would have been for Billy. Billy's terror on Cottle's account was so intense that he forgot his own injuries and struggled up to a sitting position. For a moment he went giddy and sick, but after a few minutes managed to gain his feet. He looked round. The very first thing he saw was a dead body, and a fresh pang of terror seized him.

But a second glance showed him that it was the man whom he himself had shot down, the one who had tried to knife Cottle. He set to searching round and found two other bodies, but both were those of Pecos' men. Of Cottle there was no sign at all.

" Then he's a prisoner," groaned Billy. " That reptile Pecos has got him." He braced himself and tried to think what was best to do. His head throbbed horribly and his mouth and throat were dry as leather, while his legs felt like paper. He had to confess to himself that he was in no state to start off on a rescue expedition.

Suddenly he remembered Castro. Castro was still prisoner in Copan's hands, and so long as that was the case Pecos would not dare to murder or mistreat Cottle. The thought gave Billy some comfort, and he made up his mind that the best thing he could do was to go back to the cave and consult with Copan. He started, but found himself so weak and giddy that he could only crawl. Thirst tortured him. It was worse than the pain in his head.

It came to him that probably one of the rebels had a canteen or flask, and he went back. Two bodies he examined without finding what he sought, but on the third, strapped to his belt, was a felt-covered water-bottle, and as he lifted it Billy heard a welcome gurgle within. He unscrewed the top and put it to his lips, but the first taste of the fluid was so nasty that he almost dropped it.

The water was mixed with coarse mescal or cactus brandy which had a strong flavour of turpentine. Yet evil as the taste was, Billy realised that it was better than nothing, and forced himself to take a couple of swallows. It did him good, and presently, finding that the worst of the giddiness had passed, he put the flask in one pocket, the pistol in another, and started off to search for the way down the rocks on the cliff path.

He went cautiously, and this caution saved his life. For, as he came nearer to the head of the cross-ravine, he caught a ray of moonlight reflected upon the blued barrel of a rifle. He pulled up short, and, taking cover behind a bush, peered round it in an effort to make out the identity of the man who held the gun.

The fellow moved, and Billy saw that he was one of the rebels. He was leaning on a rock close to the edge of the rift and twenty paces away; on the other side of the rift stood a second man, also armed. Billy did not need telling that these were sentries set by Pecos to bar the way up and down from the cliff path below.

He drew back into cover and considered the matter. His first impulse was, as usual, to attack. He had his pistol and thought that he might easily creep up on the nearest man and shoot him down. But the other—the other he could not reach, for the man was on the far side of the rift, and Billy had to realise that while he

was shooting at the first he would be at the mercy
of the second.

Billy was not usually given to worrying about
risks, and even now, so far as he himself was
concerned, he would have chanced it. But he
was forced to remember that it was Cottle's life
he was risking as well as his own, for if Cottle
was, as seemed certain, in Pecos' hands, he,
Billy, was the only person to free him, and the
only one who could fly the Dolphin back to
safety.

" It's no good," groaned Billy at last under
his breath. " I dare not chance it." He paused.
" Yet, if I don't, what happens?" He glanced
at the sky and noticed that the crescent moon
was now high above the hills. " Must be nearly
four," he said. " It will be daylight in two
hours. Then what am I going to do?"

It was quite clear to Billy that he had to do
something, if only to find a hiding-place before
daylight. What was more, he had not much time
to spare, for already the stars were beginning to
dim.

He looked around, but saw no hiding-place
near. Besides, he needed food and water, and
neither of these were available anywhere near.

Thought of the Dolphin flashed into his mind.
The plane was well hidden among the big buildings on the far side of the square, and in a place
where the rebels did not seem to go. There was
food, too, as well as water in the plane, and it
came to Billy that if he could reach her he could
lie up safely during the hours of daylight.

Without delay he crept away to the left. The going was bad, but he found cover all the way, and, making a big circle so as to avoid the temple, found himself at last on the western side of the great square.

He paused and looked round. There were lights in the temple, but nowhere else, and although the dawn was now showing plainly in the sky the shadow was heavy under the eaves of the buildings bounding the square. Keeping well in this shadow, Billy crept onwards.

At last he gained the massive ruins on the north side of the square. His head was still aching so badly that he stopped for a few moments to rest and look round.

While he waited he heard steps coming up behind, so forcing himself back into a niche between two broken columns he stood listening breathlessly. Sure enough someone was coming. Someone had heard him and was tracking him. A moment later he saw the man, a tall, powerfully built fellow armed with a rifle. Billy himself had no weapon except a knife, and knew that he was in no shape for a hand-to-hand fight. So he pushed himself deeper into the recess, and prayed that he might escape the notice of his enemy.

The rebel came prowling past so close that Billy could almost have touched him—so close that he could see the man's fierce face and scowling eyes. There was a moment of desperate suspense, then the fellow passed and strode silently onwards.

Twenty yards farther on was an opening

between two buildings, and Billy was almost sure that this was the one through which they had wheeled the Dolphin on the previous night. He saw the big rebel pause, then turn into this opening, and his heart sank, for if the man spotted the plane then his last hope was gone. In sheer desperation Billy drew his knife from its sheath and crept cautiously forward on the track of the ruffian.

The moment he reached the corner, Billy recognised the opening. It *was* the one through which they had pushed the plane, and in the half-light he could see the great mass of ruined building into the hollow beneath which they had hidden her. He saw, too, what he had not noticed in the darkness of the night, namely, that a luxuriant growth of dark-leafed creeper covered this building, hanging down in front of it like an immense curtain.

It was this creeper which hid the plane from view, and Billy hoped against hope that the spy would not see it. To his horror the man went on. While he could not, of course, have any idea where the plane was hidden, it was clear that he thought Billy might have concealed himself in this hiding-place, and with his rifle at the " ready " he stalked slowly forward.

Billy felt so desperate that for the moment he forgot his aches and pains. At any cost he must save his beloved Dolphin, and grasping his knife he tiptoed forward. Suddenly the rebel pulled up short, and Billy heard him give a grunt of surprise. Billy knew what had happened—he had spotted the plane through some opening in the thick foliage.

But instead of going forward the rebel stood quite still, staring fixedly in front of him. Not a breath of air was moving and the silence was so intense that Billy could actually hear the man's heavy breathing. Something else he heard. A curious rustling sound like dry leaves moving before the wind.

The sound died away, and once more all was still. Billy saw the big rebel step forward and raise one arm to push aside the heavy trails of the creeper. Next instant something like a huge rope darted out through the opening and with incredible swiftness wrapped itself round the man's body. Billy heard a cry, smothered almost before it was uttered, and with a shock of horror realised that the rebel was in the grip of a monstrous snake.

He dashed forward, but, quick as he was, before he could reach the spot there was a horrid crunching sound and man and snake dropped together and rolled upon the ground. Sick with horror, Billy slashed furiously at a shining coil, striking with such force that his blade shore right through the tightly stretched body of the great reptile.

Before he knew what was happening Billy himself was knocked sprawling, and leaves and dust were flung in every direction in the death agony of the giant python. Half-stunned, it was some moments before Billy could collect himself, and when he did at last regain his feet only a few convulsive movements showed that there was any life left in the monster.

But if the snake was dead so was the man, and it seemed to Billy that every bone in the wretched fellow's body had been broken. There was nothing to be done, so, stepping cautiously over the corpses, Billy entered the dark recess between the curtain of creeper and the ancient wall. The plane was there just as he and Cottle had left it, but before going any farther Billy had a good look round in order to make sure that there was not a second snake in the place.

But nothing moved, nor were there any signs of life, and presently Billy ventured to climb up into the body of the Dolphin and help himself to a sorely needed drink of water. By this time the light was increasing rapidly, and Billy saw that the first thing he must do was to conceal the bodies of the man and the snake.

It taxed his strength to drag them in under cover, but he managed it at last, and finding a deep crack in the ground a little way off, pushed them both into this ready-made tomb. Then, completely worn out, he climbed back into the plane, stretched himself, and fell asleep.

CHAPTER TWENTY-ONE

GREEN STONES

THE sun was high in the sky when Billy woke, and judging by the shadows it was past midday. Billy himself felt much the better for his sleep.

Climbing out he parted the hanging branches and glanced towards the square, but all was quiet. Somewhat relieved, Billy went back to the plane, lighted a spirit lamp and put on a coffee-pot. While this was boiling he washed the wound on his head and bandaged it.

Having made a good meal, he felt more like himself and decided to see if he could repair the plane. To put in the spare magneto was a longish job, but not one that presented any particular difficulties to so good a mechanic as Billy.

For nearly three hours Billy was desperately busy. Not only did he put in the spare magneto, but he went over the whole engine, and by the time he had finished felt fairly convinced that the Dolphin would fly as well as ever she had.

It gave Billy immense satisfaction to feel that the Dolphin was herself again, for now, if he could only manage to rescue Cottle, they had ready their means of escape. But Cottle, so Billy believed, was a prisoner in the hands of Pecos, and rack his brains as he might he could not think of any means of getting him free.

While he struggled vainly for some plan the sun set and the short tropical dusk settled over the ruined city. The heat was great, and once or twice Billy heard a rumble of thunder.

By this time he was hungry again, so he boiled up some more coffee, opened a tin of meat and made a hearty supper. As he ate the thunder rolled again, but now it sounded as if it were underground instead of from the sky. Then all of a sudden the earth beneath him heaved slightly and Billy realised that this was his first experience of what South Americans call the "tremblor."

Presently it was dark, and Billy, unable longer to stand the suspense of waiting, decided to go out and scout. As before, he kept well under the buildings on the western side of the square, but now he was less nervous than he had been, for he was well armed and had his pockets full of ammunition and food. His idea was to get as near as possible to the temple, hide, and try if he could overhear anything that would give him a clue to Cottle's whereabouts. Moving very cautiously, he got right round to the back of the temple and was searching for a suitable hiding-place when he caught a slight rustling in some bushes at a little distance. Next moment a tall, lean figure crept out of the bushes and, bent double, came straight forward towards the spot where Billy had dropped and was lying flat on the ground.

Billy's rifle went to his shoulder. "Stop, or I'll blow your head off!" he said curtly.

" Not mine, Billy," was the astonishing reply, and Billy, hardly able to believe his senses, knew the voice for Cottle's.

" I—I thought you were a prisoner!" gasped Billy.

" Same here, old man," replied Cottle. " Then I suppose we were both on the same job—each looking for the other. But, Billy, my lad, this isn't exactly a health resort. Follow me and I'll take you to a spot where we can talk in something like safety."

Bent double, Cottle slipped silently away in a westerly direction until they reached a secluded spot hidden by thick bushes. " This is good enough," said Cottle, seating himself on a lump of stone and making room for Billy beside him. " Billy, boy, I can't tell you how pleased I am to see you. What a brute you must have thought me to desert you in that fashion."

" I didn't think anything of the sort," replied Billy indignantly. " I felt sure Pecos had got you."

" Someone got me," said Cottle ruefully— " got me a crack on the head and laid me out. When I came to I found myself in the cave. Copan and his merry men had somehow dragged me there, but not one of them knew what had become of you."

" Like you, I got knocked out," said Billy. " When I came to I was all alone."

" Rotten for you," said Cottle with sympathy. " How did you manage, old chap?"

Billy told the story of his adventures of the

previous night. When he came to the way in which the great snake had destroyed the rebel Cottle interrupted him. " I half thought there might have been a snake there. As a matter of fact I believe I heard the brute while we were hiding the plane. Those big pythons make a curious snoring sound when they're asleep." He paused. " Billy," he added gravely, " I should never have forgiven myself if the creature had got you instead of the rebel."

" It turned out all right as it was," said Billy. " I've mended the plane," he continued. " I put in the spare magneto, and I believe she'll fly as well as ever. Don't you think the best thing we can do is to get away as soon as possible? We know now where the green gold comes from, and we've put Castro where he can do no more harm."

Cottle nodded. " I quite agree with all you say, Billy, but we can't start yet. You see, Pecos has more than a notion of where we have been hiding, and if he or his men find a way down to the cave, that spells our finish. The rebels would get Castro back, and, not only that, they would find any quantity more of the gold."

" And they'd scupper poor old Copan and all his crowd," said Billy ruefully.

" There's no doubt about that," agreed Cottle, " and it wouldn't be playing the game to desert them."

" That's true," said Billy slowly. " Copan has been a very good friend to us."

" You don't know how good," Cottle told

him. "Look at this." As he spoke he took from
his pocket something wrapped in a scrap of paper
and handed it to Billy. Billy's eyes widened, for
even in the dim starlight he saw that the object
was an emerald of such size and colour as he had
never before imagined.

"Phew! It must be worth a fortune!" he
exclaimed.

"All of a thousand pounds," replied Cottle,
" and Copan has bags of them. Emeralds, Billy,
are far more portable than gold, and far more
valuable, for at present there are hardly any on
the market. If we could take a pocketful of these
back to the President he would no longer need
to worry about the oilfields, and he could buy
planes and guns enough to mop up the rebels in
a month."

Billy sat silent for a moment or two. "Then
what do you suggest doing, sir?" he asked at
last. "How are we going to collect Castro and
this bunch of gems? I suppose the ledge is still
guarded?" He stopped short. "How did you
get up?"

"I climbed up through the rift," said Cottle
quietly.

"Through the rift," repeated Billy in astonishment, "but Pecos had posted two sentries at the
top."

"They were there all right," smiled Cottle.
"Luckily I still had one of my little 'sleep'
bombs. It was the last of the bunch, and I hated
to use it, but it did the trick to perfection, and

two perfectly good rebels are at present lying like logs in one of the underground prisons."

"Then we can get down the same way!" exclaimed Billy eagerly.

"I don't see why not," replied Cottle. "It strikes me the sooner we start the better. What with bringing Castro back up the cliff and lugging him to where the plane is hidden, we have a busy night before us."

Billy raised his head and peered cautiously over a low bush. For some moments he stared hard in the direction of the black gap that was the entrance to the ravine. Then he ducked down again.

"I can't see a thing, sir," he whispered to Cottle.

"Then apparently Pecos has not discovered the loss of his two sentries," smiled Cottle. "Come on, Billy."

Side by side the two crept across the narrow piece of ground that separated them from the edge of the rift. "It's too easy," was the thought that came into Billy's mind, and just then he heard a faint rustle behind him. Before he could so much as turn, a man leaped out of the bushes upon his back and bore him down, flat on his face, on the rock.

Half-stunned as he was he struggled furiously, but a second man joined the first and their combined weight flattened him out completely. Close by he heard a pistol crack, a scream, and a shout of "*O Santo Dios.*"

" *Bestias!* Fools! Hold him, can't you?" came Pecos' voice, harsh and angry.

" We have him, *capitaz*," answered one of his men hoarsely, " but he has shot Josef."

" More fool you to let him," snarled Pecos. " Tie them tightly. We're not taking any more chances with these cursed Inglese."

Billy's hands were wrenched round behind his back, and a strip of rawhide knotted hard around his wrists. Then he was jerked to his feet. A lantern, held by one of the rebels, showed him Cottle as helpless as himself, while in front of them stood Pecos, his ugly yellow face alight with evil triumph.

" You thought yourselves so clever," he sneered, " but your brains do not match those of Juan Pecos. It was I who set the trap into which you have walked so foolishly."

" I suppose you had to get a bit of your own back, Pecos," jeered Billy. " Do you remember how sick you were that day you looped the loop?"

An expression of almost fiendish malice convulsed Pecos' face, and, stepping forward, he struck Billy across the mouth. Next instant the rebel chief went flying backwards into the bushes. If Billy's hands were tied, his feet were still at liberty, and he knew how to make good use of them.

" Look out, Billy," cried Cottle warningly. " He will shoot you for that." For the moment it seemed that Cottle's words would come true, for as Pecos came clambering back out of the bush into which he had been kicked his little eyes were blazing with insane fury, and his right hand was grasping for the butt of his pistol.

One of his men interfered. " Pardon, *capitaz*," he said. " The dog deserves death, but you yourself warned us to take them both alive."

Pecos lowered his pistol. " You are right, Almagro," he answered in a queer, grating voice. " It would be wasting them to shoot them out of hand. But they shall pay. *Por Dios*, they shall pay."

" Take them to the armoury," he said after a short pause. " Take them straight to the armoury, and remember that your lives are forfeit if they escape."

Their captors hurried them along, and within a few minutes Billy and Cottle found themselves standing against the wall in the big room on the ground floor of the temple. Pecos, stalking in behind them, seated himself on a bench opposite. " Tie their legs," he ordered, and this was done.

For some moments Pecos sat staring at them, a look of gratified malice on his ugly face. But Cottle's intensely blue eyes bored straight into his mottled brown ones, and Pecos' gaze fell.

" What about it?" said Cottle quietly. " Now that you have got us, Pecos, what are you going to do with us? I feel sure you would like to murder us, but I don't think you dare to so long as Castro is in our power."

Pecos' lips twisted in a wolf-like snarl. " But I have two prisoners," he retorted, " while you only have one. Listen to me: I will give you one chance to save your miserable lives. My terms are these. You will restore to us our General, you will hand over your aeroplane, and you will deliver to me the secret of the entrance to the caves of the Chiapas."

Cottle smiled. "You don't want much, do you, Pecos?" he answered in his perfect Spanish. "And what will you do if we refuse to fall in with your pleasant plans?"

"Refuse?" repeated Pecos savagely. "Refuse, and you shall learn how a son of Spain treats his enemies."

"You flatter yourself, Pecos. Spain would not own you."

Pecos sprang up almost foaming, but Cottle did not move an inch. He cursed Cottle savagely, but Cottle never turned a hair—merely watched him with a disdainful smile.

Exhausted with rage, Pecos turned at last to his lieutenant, Almagro. "Take them to the upper room," he ordered. "Leave them there upon the floor. We will see what twenty-four hours without food or water will do for these proud ones."

Almagro signed to some of his men, and these, picking up the two prisoners, swung them off their feet, and carried them up a flight of broken stone stairs into a low-roofed upper room where they dumped them unceremoniously on the floor.

Almagro stood over them. "It is hot here when the sun shines," he said grimly, then he turned away and left them.

Billy drew a long breath. " It's something to be rid of the smell of them," he said.

But Cottle's face was grave. " Almagro was right, Billy," he said. " It will be hot here when the sun shines."

Billy felt that he was right, for even now in the darkness the air was stifling, but he refused to be discouraged. " I'm going to try to sleep," he said quietly.

CHAPTER TWENTY-TWO

THE BRONZE BLADE

IN spite of the heat, in spite of his aching wrists and ankles, Billy did manage to sleep. Cramp woke him and he roused to find the rising sun shining through the narrow windows. Looking round he saw Cottle, propped against the wall, watching him.

" How do you feel, Billy?" he asked.

" I'm all right," said Billy bravely, as he twisted and wriggled to straighten his tangled muscles. " No one's been near us, I suppose?"

" No, nor likely to," replied Cottle grimly. " Master Pecos meant what he said last night."

" I suppose there's no chance of Copan being able to help us out?" said Billy, licking his dry lips."

" Not much, I'm afraid," responded Cottle. " He can't get at us up here."

" Then it's up to us to help ourselves," said Billy.

" Quite so," agreed Cottle. " If we could get our hands free, we might do something. But I've no knife, and I see they've taken yours."

" If we could only find a sharp stone some-where," suggested Billy, but Cottle shook his head.

" That's what I have been looking for ever since daylight, but there's nothing of the sort within reach. If we had that knife up there, it would be distinctly useful."

Billy glanced up at the wall at which Cottle was gazing and saw a strange old bronze knife hanging against it. "Can't we get it?" he exclaimed eagerly.

"I've tried, Billy," said Cottle. "I have tried every way I knew, but I am certain that it is quite out of the question."

Billy lay quiet for some moments, staring at the knife. It was maddening to see it there and realise that, if it were within reach, it would give them a means of escape. Yet he had to own that Cottle was right and that there was no way of getting it.

The sun rose and every minute the heat increased. Soon both prisoners were suffering tortures from thirst. Down below they could hear the rebels stirring, talking together as they cooked their breakfast. A rich scent of boiling coffee rose through the cracks in the broken floor.

Presently there were steps on the stone staircase, and Pecos himself arrived, followed by a man who carried two great mugs of coffee. "Good-morning, señores," said Pecos with his twisted grin. "By this time you have, no doubt, repented of your foolish defiance of last night, and are ready to give me the information which I require. In return, I shall be pleased to present you with your breakfast and your liberty."

"You go to blazes," growled Billy, but Cottle checked him.

"Steady, Billy, don't be rude to the gentleman." Then he addressed himself to Pecos. "No, Señor Pecos. While we are obliged for your kind offer, we should wish you to understand that Englishmen are not accustomed to betray their friends. I am afraid you will have to wait a little longer before we change our minds."

Fury convulsed Pecos' ugly face, but he checked himself. "It is well, Señor Cottle. I can afford to wait better than you. A thunderstorm is brewing, and the heat is increasing. The temperature here should be well over a hundred by midday. Sooner or later you are bound to cry for mercy." He turned to his man. "Take the coffee away, Pedro; the señores are not yet ready for their breakfast."

Pecos was right in his weather prophecy. A thunderstorm was brewing. The atmosphere became more and more sultry, and the heat in this upper place was like that of a furnace. Thirst tortured Billy. It seemed to him that he would willingly give all the rest of his life for one glass of cold water.

The sunlight faded to a coppery glow, but the heat did not diminish. Indeed, it seemed to increase, and Billy and Cottle were both panting for breath. It seemed to Billy that he had been years, instead of hours, in this horrible prison.

The torture under which he was suffering was so intense that he was becoming light-headed. The yellow gloom grew thicker. Then the darkness was pierced by a flash of white fire, and there followed a roll of thunder so heavy that the whole great temple quivered. Another flash, another boom, then with a roar louder than the thunder itself the heavens opened and down came the rain.

Since arriving in San Lucar, Billy had seen more than one tropical thunderstorm, but all had been as child's play to the present tempest. So terrific was the rain that it broke through cracks in the massive roof of the temple, and the next thing Billy knew he was lying in a pool of water.

Rolling over on his face, he licked up the dusty fluid with delight, and with each gulp felt strength come back into him.

" Feeling better, Billy?" came a quiet question from Cottle, and Billy flushed with shame to think that for the moment he had actually forgotten his friend.

" It's all right, old chap," smiled Cottle, " I was just as bad as you, and I think the pool I found was a little the deeper." Before Billy could reply, there came such a peal of thunder that, for the moment, it seemed as though the whole temple was going to fall to pieces.

It was like the explosion of a magazine, and, for the moment, left both Billy and Cottle stunned and deafened. In the momentary silence that followed Cottle spoke.

" Billy," he said, and there was a curious ring in his voice, " look at the wall!"

Billy looked. He gasped. Then, regardless of the pools of water lying in every hollow, he began to roll frantically over and over in the direction of the wall. For he saw, as Cottle had already seen, that the tremendous vibration had loosened the precious knife, and that it was now lying on the floor beneath the spot where it had been hanging.

Bronze does not rust like steel, and when he reached the knife Billy found that the edge was still as keen as at the time, perhaps centuries earlier, when it had first been made.

Squirming round, he got the handle between his teeth and sat up. Next moment he heard Cottle's voice close beside him. "Quite a useful-looking article," remarked the Professor. "Now, if Master Pecos does not interfere, we may have a surprise in store for him. Drop the knife, Billy, then turn round with your back to me."

Cottle's fingers were long and flexible, and although his hands were swollen and stiff from the bonds, yet he managed to get the edge of the blade against the thong of rawhide between Billy's wrists, and so set to sawing it through. The stuff was almost as tough as wire and the job was a long and difficult one.

Both Billy and Cottle were in a state of great suspense for fear Pecos or any of his men might appear, but the great storm still rattled and crashed above the ruined city, and none of the rebels ventured up the crazy stairs.

Presently came Cottle's voice in his ear: "That's done the trick, Billy," and even as he spoke, Billy felt the harsh reins drop away from his aching wrists.

Five minutes steady rubbing and another

drink of water from one of the pools on the floor left the two prisoners almost as good as new. The worst of the thunderstorm was over, but the rain was still roaring down with unabated force, pounding so heavily on the roof as to drown all other sounds.

"What do we do now, sir?" asked Billy briskly.

"That's a bit of a problem," Cottle answered. "I think that the best thing is to wait where we are until Pecos shows up again, then collar him and hold him to ransom."

Billy looked doubtful. "That may mean hours of waiting," he objected. "Couldn't we creep half-way down the stairs and see what's happening below?"

Cottle considered for a moment. "It might be a good idea," he agreed, "but we mustn't risk being spotted. Wait here, Billy, while I try it."

"That's mean of you, sir," complained Billy, "seeing that it was my idea." But Cottle was already on the stairs and moving downwards with swift silence. Billy crouched at the top, waiting in great suspense. He saw Cottle reach the bend and peer over into the depths below. For more than a minute Cottle remained there motionless, then turned and came creeping cautiously back. His face was very grave as he rejoined Billy. "What's up?" asked Billy breathlessly.

"They've got Copan," was Cottle's brief reply.

Billy bit off a startled exclamation: " Copan? What was he doing there?"

" He must have come to look for us," Cottle explained.

" Then they'll force him to give up Castro," said Billy in great dismay.

" They won't," replied Cottle briefly. " The little man is staunch as they make them."

" Then they will probably bring him up here and put him with us," said Billy.

" If they do, the fat's in the fire," remarked Cottle, " but steady a minute, Billy, I'll go down and have another look."

" Then I'm coming, too," declared Billy. " I can't stick it up here all alone."

" No," said Cottle firmly. " You wait at the head of the stairs. But, if I beckon, you can follow."

Down went Cottle again, while Billy waited with even greater anxiety than before. Two minutes dragged by, each seeming as long as an hour. Then, at last, Billy saw Cottle turn and beckon. Another moment and he was by his side.

The spot where Cottle was crouching was hidden from sight of any one in the great room below. Cottle did not speak, merely pointed. Looking down, Billy was puzzled by what he saw, for the whole force of rebels, with Pecos and Copan at their head, were filing out through the broken door leading down into the sloping passage. Two sentries, only, were left behind.

There was dismay on Billy's face as he turned

to Cottle. " Copan has given in," he whispered. " Pecos has got round him."

" It may look like it," replied Cottle in an equally low voice, " but I don't believe it is so. Little Copan is a white man, and my belief is that he has still a trick up his sleeve."

" You mean that he might lead them into some blind passage?" suggested Billy.

" Something of the sort," agreed Cottle. " I am quite sure he would think nothing of his own life if he could finish up the rebels."

" What are we going to do?"

" Go, too, I think," replied Cottle calmly. " There's no hurry, son. We must let Pecos & Co. get a bit of a start before we tackle those sentries."

Quivering with impatience, Billy waited until Pecos' whole force had filed away down the passage. Some of the men were carrying torches, the smoky glare of which faded slowly into the darkness. The two sentries stood close to the mouth of the passage watching the departure of their comrades.

Cottle turned to Billy. " There are rifles in that rack close to the foot of the stairs," he said. " If we can get a couple before the sentries spot us, we should be able to hold them up. But remember, Billy, there must be no shooting, and no noise."

On tiptoe, silent as two cats, the pair stole downwards. It was a touchy business, for, if the sentries turned, they were bound to see them. Fortunately, the men were too engrossed in watching the passage, and the Englishmen gained the foot of the stairs and the arms rack without being noticed.

Very softly Cottle slipped a rifle from the rack and raised it to his shoulder and Billy did the same. The two guards were still gazing down the passage, and outside the rain still drummed upon the square. Still Cottle did not speak, but step by step moved across the paved floor, until the muzzle of his rifle almost touched the head of the nearest guard.

" Hands up!" he remarked quietly. " Pronto!"

The man whirled. His yellow face went livid and his knees trembled so that he almost fell. His companion, threatened by Billy's rifle, was equally terrified. Small wonder, for to their superstitious minds the sight of these two Englishmen, whom they, themselves, had seen firmly tied up and imprisoned on the previous night, savoured of witchcraft.

Neither made any attempt at resistance, and in a couple of minutes they were tied and gagged and laid away in a far corner of the room.

" Take your rifle," said Cottle, " and as many cartridges as you can stuff in your pockets."

" Just what I was thinking," said Billy, as he packed one clip after another into the pockets of his jacket.

Cottle hurried away down the passage and Billy followed. The glare of the torches was already fading in the distance, and the first thing of which Billy became aware was that Copan had not betrayed the position of the secret door, but was leading the rebels straight down the main passage.

"Where does this go?" Billy whispered to Cottle.

"I wish I knew," was the answer. "But I think it must come out on the ledge somewhere lower down."

"I believe you are right," said Billy, "and that Copan has something up his sleeve."

"I hope so, indeed," replied Cottle earnestly. "Go steady, Billy," he added; "whatever happens, we mustn't let them see us."

There was not really much risk of the rebels seeing the two Englishmen, as the latter were carrying no lights, and the torches carried by Pecos' men showed only a dull, red glare. Still, the light was enough for Billy and Cottle to be able to see Copan walking alongside Pecos at the head of the party.

"This passage is different from the others," Billy whispered in Cottle's ear. "Look what a dip there is just ahead, and see how it rises again beyond."

"I expect it was a water-lock," Cottle answered. "A place they were able to flood so's to stop their enemies from following."

"There's no water there now," said Billy. As he spoke, Copan and Pecos began to descend into the curious dip, and the rest of the party followed.

CHAPTER TWENTY-THREE

THE POISON POOL

THIS part of the passage was somewhat ruinous. Earthquakes in past times had broken away portions of the roof, and just ahead of Cottle and Billy, and between them and the rebels, a mass of fallen boulders blocked half the passage, partly cutting off their view of those ahead.

They quickened their pace slightly in order not to lose sight of Pecos, but before they reached the fall Billy gave a low-voiced exclamation. " It's getting dark," he muttered.

Next moment came a queer, muffled cry. " There's something up," gasped Billy, and was hurrying forward when Cottle caught him by the arm and pulled him into the shelter of the fallen stones. " You are right," he whispered, " there is something up. This seems a good place to wait and find out what it is."

Pecos' voice rang out harsh and shrill. " Stop him! Stop him, you fool!"

" Copan's bolted," panted Billy. " I say, all the torches are going out. What has happened?"

Cottle peered round the corner of the fall. " You are right, Billy. There are only about a couple of torches left alight, and, by the row that is going on, those dagoes are scared stiff."

He paused an instant, then suddenly caught Billy and dragged him back close against the wall. " They're coming back," he muttered. " They are running for their lives."

A moment later the rebels, led by the only two whose torches were still alight, came charging back up the passage in blind panic. Their heavy boots clattered on the stone floor, they panted and sobbed as they ran. Jammed in the centre of them was Pecos. He was not scared. On the contrary, he was raging with anger, and was striking at every one he could reach with a stick which he carried.

They paid no more attention to him than if he had been a mosquito, but swept him onwards in their headlong flight. Not one of them gave a glance towards the two Englishmen who crouched against the wall in the angle of the fall.

In a matter of seconds the whole mob was past, and sweeping back towards the guard-room. Billy gazed after them. " What happened?" he demanded of Cottle. " What sort of stunt did Copan put up? How did the rum little beggar get away from them?"

" You ought to know, Billy," said Cottle gently. " It was you who spotted that dip in the passage."

" The dip?" repeated Billy slowly.

" Yes," said Cottle. " You pointed out that there was no water in it, but it evidently held something else."

" Gas," replied Billy sharply. " Carbonic acid gas."

"Exactly," said Cottle. "A pool of it. Without a doubt Copan knew all about it, and bolted through without breathing, but the rebels blundered into it and were, of course, scared stiff when their torches went out. No doubt they put it down to witchcraft, and Pecos will have a job to get hold of them again."

Billy chuckled under his breath. "Good old Copan! But I say, Professor, he must know of some bolt hole at the far end of this place."

"Not a doubt of it," said Cottle, "and the sooner we follow him the better."

"That's all very well," replied Billy, "but how are we going to find our way? It's as black as a hat."

"That can be remedied," said Cottle. "Luckily I have a few loose matches which those beggars didn't find when they searched me, and the chances are that there are plenty of torches lying about."

"Then let's get ahead," said Billy eagerly. "There's not a rebel left in sight."

Cottle listened a moment but, as Billy had said, there was no sign of their enemies. Next moment there was the scratch of a match, and a small blue flame illuminated the darkness. Billy swooped forward. "Here's a torch," he exclaimed. "Why, the place is stiff with them."

"Rifles too," added Cottle. "Those dagoes were properly panic-stricken." As he spoke he lighted the torch, which flared up with a red blaze. "Put your handkerchief over your mouth," he told Billy, "while you go through

237

the dip. I shall hold the torch as high as I can and try to keep it above the level of the choke-damp."

Next minute the two were in the dip. Both had stopped their mouths and nostrils, and Cottle, leading the way, held the torch at the full reach of his long right arm. At the lowest point of the dip the flame dulled for a moment but did not quite go out, then, as the ground rose again, the resinous wood blazed up afresh. A few strides more and they were out of the hollow and the pool of deadly gas which it contained.

"That's good," said Billy, drawing a long breath. "The question now is where Copan has got to."

"A question that need not trouble you much," said Cottle dryly, and as he spoke the white-robed figure of the Chiapa chief stepped out from a deep niche in one side of the passage.

"I greet you, friends," he said in his precise Spanish. "Happy am I that you have escaped from those wicked ones."

Billy grasped his hand delightedly. "It was you who turned the trick, chief," he grinned. "He means," explained Cottle, "that it was your cleverness, chief, which put the rebels to flight."

"It was simple," replied Copan modestly, "seeing that I only knew of the pool of bad air. But now come quickly, for it may be that the man Pecos has knowledge to understand. This passage leadeth to the ledge, and soon ye will be safe in the great cave."

It was a delight to Cottle and Billy to find themselves once more in the open, breathing the fresh, rain-washed air. It was still more pleasant to find themselves in the cave, welcomed by the kindly Chiapas and enjoying a much-needed meal. Copan sat with them while they ate, and the three talked over their plans.

Billy was urgent that they must get Castro out at once before Pecos had time to rally his men. " But we can't cross the square in broad daylight," objected Cottle.

" There is no need to," replied Billy. " My notion is to bridge the gap in the ledge, rush the guards at the upper end, and take the passage leading to the centre of the square. Then we simply bolt for the plane and are up and away before the rebels can start shooting."

" Why not wait till night, Billy?" suggested Cottle.

" Because by that time Pecos will have got things in hand again. He will have his guards out all over the place. Besides, it would be a precious awkward job to rise out of that square in darkness."

Cottle shrugged his shoulders. " You know best, Billy. Let us go."

A dull roar made the rock floor beneath them quiver. Billy sprang up and ran for the entrance. A moment later he was back. " We're done," he said grimly. " That confounded thunderstorm has come back. It's begun to blow like blazes. I could never get the plane up in such a gale.

Cottle hurried out of the cave, but was back in a minute. "It's bad, Billy, I'll admit," he said, "but, after all, I don't suppose it will last. This is what I suggest: that we go up the path and try to make our way through the passage to the square; then hide in the ruins and wait for the storm to pass. In one way the bad weather will help us, for Pecos will never dream of our starting out in it. In any case, Billy, if we can get Castro and the emeralds safe to Las Cruces, our job is finished. Castro is the brain of the whole outfit, and without him the rebellion will very soon go phut."

"I'm sure you're right, sir," Billy answered. "Then the sooner we get along the better."

A few minutes later, when the little party started up the ledge, the storm was raging furiously again. Rain fell in torrents, and great gusts of wind roared down the ravine. Cottle led the way, then came Castro, with his hands tied and gagged so that he could not cry out. Billy followed, and last came Copan.

Cottle had wished Copan to remain behind, for, as he had told the chief, it was impossible to take him in the plane, but the plucky little man had insisted on coming, declaring that he could find his own way back to the cave.

The gap had been bridged, and they crossed it without trouble, but it was ticklish work making their way up the ledge in the teeth of the raging gale. As they neared the entrance to the tunnel leading to the square Cottle paused and signed to Billy to stop. Then he himself went cautiously forward.

In a moment or two he was back. "Not a sign of a guard, Billy," he said. "The weather must have driven them inside."

The event proved Cottle to have been perfectly right, for Pecos' two sentries had wrapped themselves in their cloaks and were squatting down inside the passage, with their backs against the walls, smoking black cigarettes. So great was the shock when the two Englishmen sprang in out of the storm on top of them that neither attempted to put up any fight. They did not even shout for help.

It was a matter of moments before they were both tied and gagged and rolled aside into a recess.

"Almost too easy," said Billy as they pushed on up the passage.

"Don't let that worry you, Billy," said Cottle dryly. "We have trouble enough to come before we get away from Sanat."

They were all eyes and ears as they advanced along the tunnel, yet there was not a trace of any of Pecos' men, and even when they reached the end of the passage, where the hidden door opened under the statue into the square, there was nothing to interfere with them.

The door was closed. Copan stepped forward and began to weight the counter-poise, but when he had put the stones into position nothing happened. The door did not move. "I knew there was a catch somewhere," growled Billy. "What are we going to do now, Professor?"

"We have still a stick of dynamite," replied Cottle calmly.

Billy's eyes widened. "But the explosion will bring the whole crowd out of the temple," he remonstrated.

"Not in this," answered Cottle, and even as he spoke the solid rock beneath them trembled under the bellowing vibration of a thunderclap.

Billy looked relieved. "All right, sir," he said, and set to fixing the charge against the door. "Better get well back," he said. "You never quite know what dynamite will do in a confined space like this."

Cottle nodded and moved back up the passage. Next moment Billy joined them, and all four pressed themselves closely against the wall and waited. They had not long to wait. Within a few seconds came the heavy thump of the exploding dynamite, followed by a rending, crashing sound. A wave of air rushed back up the passage, and the solid floor rocked beneath them.

Billy leaped to his feet and ran forward. "It's all right," he called joyfully.

So far as the door went, it was certainly all right, for the dynamite had smashed the great stone slab to atoms, but the force of the explosion had flung pieces outwards and they lay scattered in confusion in the square outside.

So long as the storm lasted these would not be noticed, but Cottle realised that when it passed the fragments could hardly escape the rebels' notice. However, it was no use worrying about that. The thing was to get across the square as quickly as possible and find some hiding-place not too far from the plane.

So, lugging the reluctant Castro between them, Cottle and Billy hurried through the opening and out into the driving storm.

" Those houses to the left," Billy said to Cottle, and pointed. " I'm pretty sure I know a good place to hide." At the moment that he spoke there came one of those curious pauses which so often occur in a tropical thunderstorm. For a moment the rain ceased as completely as though a tap had been turned off.

" Look out," said Cottle. " That means a big flash." The words were hardly out of his mouth before it came.

A blinding, blue-white glare lit up the whole square like a magnesium flare and was accompanied by a crack of thunder like the explosion of a thousand powder barrels. Then down came the rain again, hissing like smoke off the streaming ground.

" That's done it," said Billy in dismay. " I say, Professor, they can hardly have helped seeing us."

" I'm half-afraid you are right, Billy," Cottle answered, and broke into a run. Through the hiss of the rain came a sharp crackling sound.

" I told you so," gasped Billy, " they're shooting."

" Never mind. We shall be under cover in another minute," Cottle answered. " In any case, it will be a miracle if they hit us in this light.''

The point for which Billy was making was the opening at the end of which the plane was hidden. His original idea had been to hide behind the creepers which covered the Dolphin, but now that the rebels had spotted them he had to change his plans. To the left of the street was the great block of ruins under which he had had his encounter with the two rebels on the previous night, and he remembered a doorway leading into this building.

Making straight for this, he hauled Castro through it and was followed by Cottle and Copan. They found themselves in a vast square hall, with walls of the same massive masonry as those of the temple opposite. But the great earthquake which had destroyed the city had brought down a large part of the roof, and a mass of rubble half-blocked the floor of the place.

Billy looked anxiously around, but could see no opening anywhere in the surrounding walls except the doorway through which they had come. A look of dismay crossed his face. '' This is no use!'' he gasped. '' It is a regular trap.''

CHAPTER TWENTY-FOUR

THE VULTURES

BILLY swung round towards the door, but Copan caught his arm and began to speak in such rapid Spanish that Billy could not get the sense of his words. Cottle explained. " It is all right, Billy. The little man knows this place and a way out of it. He says there is a hole in that right-hand wall, and a place behind it where we can hide."

" He's a topper!" exclaimed Billy. " But where is this opening? The sooner we're through it the better, for here come the rebels."

He was right, for by the clatter of many feet on the pavement it was plain that a strong force was hurrying across the square. Copan glided forward and the others followed.

He led them round behind a mass of fallen masonry and there in the north wall was an opening just big enough for a man to squeeze through. Cottle was the first to enter, then Billy pushed Castro through and followed. Copan came last.

They found themselves in a second chamber, smaller than the first, but also sounder. This room still had a roof on it. There had once been a door at the western end, but the arch had fallen in. Light and air entered through a narrow window set rather high in the eastern wall.

" This is top-hole!" declared Billy delightedly. " The good Pecos will have his work cut out to find us here, and we can see all that goes on through that window."

" You are talking a whole lot," said Cottle dryly. " Suppose you save some of your breath and help us to block that opening."

Billy got rather red, and swinging up a lump of stone set to helping to make the entrance secure. They had barely finished the work before they heard Pecos' voice in the street outside. Billy rolled a stone under the window and, climbup on it, peered cautiously over the sill.

" Here they come," he said. " More than a score of them. Pecos is leading them." He ducked down. " I say, I'd love to plug him," he said to Cottle, " but I suppose it would not be quite playing the game."

" Don't be an ass, Billy," said Cottle. " How long do you think we should last once you started shooting out of that window? They'd dynamite us out of here inside five minutes."

Pecos' harsh voice came to their ears. " Spread out, men, and search the buildings on both sides. They came this way. I saw them myself."

Obeying their leader, the rebels spread out, and next minute the fugitives heard some of them in the big room which they had just left.

" That won't do them much good!" grinned Billy, and sure enough Pecos' men soon gave up the search and filed out again into the street. Billy peeped out a second time. It still rained, but the worst of the storm was over and it was growing lighter. The sun, now low in the west, was beginning to break through the mirk.

The men who had been searching in the buildings on the opposite side had, of course, been equally unsuccessful, and their leader was growing very angry.

" *Bestias!*" he shouted. " Idiots! You must find them. They cannot be far off."

Billy, delighted at Pecos' discomfiture, was still watching, when a flapping of heavy wings attracted his attention and he saw two huge buzzards rise heavily from among the bushes at the end of the street. Pecos saw them too, and was quick to realise what the birds meant.

Cottle heard Billy gasp. " What's the matter?" he demanded in a quick whisper.

" Those confounded vultures!" exclaimed Billy. " Two have come up from the bushes just beyond where the Dolphin is hidden. They've been feeding on the snake I killed. If the rebels search they'll find it and the man the snake finished."

" And then they will find the plane," added Cottle swiftly.

" They are bound to," said Billy in a fright. " Yes, Pecos is sending some men forward to search. I say, Professor, this is rotten luck."

Billy's worst fears were justified. Barely a minute later a triumphant yell announced the discovery of the Dolphin. Billy saw Pecos hurry forward. The trails of the creeper were slashed away with machetes, the heavy cutlasses carried by the rebels, and the plane exposed to view.

" Here is the flying machine," said a big rebel, " but the Inglese are not here."

Pecos was almost dancing with excitement. " It does not matter," he exclaimed, " for without the aeroplane they cannot escape. Set a guard over it. Eight men, sergeant. Four to be relieved every two hours."

Billy slipped down from the window. " That's torn it!" he said in a despairing tone. " What are we going to do now, sir?" he asked.

" I haven't the faintest idea, Billy," Cottle answered. " For the present there is nothing for it but to sit tight and wait for sunset."

While they talked in whispers the search continued. More than once men came into the big room behind them, and presently Billy, looking out again through the window, saw rebels on the opposite roofs.

The storm rolled away into the distance, but as the sky cleared the light faded, and soon the quick tropical darkness fell upon the ruined city. With it came silence.

" They've chucked it," said Billy softly. " Professor, I have been thinking. Suppose I were to slip out and creep away to some distance then fire two or three shots. It would start the guards running towards the sound and give us a chance to bolt for the plane. If we could get to her we could use her machine-gun, and you could keep the rebels off while I got her under way."

Cottle did not like the idea, but Copan when he heard of it was suddenly eager. He, however, would not hear of Billy acting as decoy, but said that he should take one of the pistols and do the firing.

"There is no need for me to come back to you, my friends," he explained, "nor will those wicked ones capture me, for they cannot follow me through the hidden paths with which I am acquainted."

Even Cottle could find no objection to this plan, and after a time they began to take the stones down from the opening. They cleared them away silently, then Cottle handed Copan the pistol.

"And now I will say farewell to you, my English friends," said the plucky little man. "Some day, perchance, we may meet again, but whether we do or no, neither my people nor myself will forget you."

"Good-bye, old scout," said Billy, gripping Copan's hand. "Good-bye and good luck to you."

"And now I will go," said Copan simply, and, silent as a ghost, slipped through the opening.

"I do hope he will be all right," whispered Billy as the other disappeared in the thick gloom. The words had hardly left his lips before there came a click and a beam of strong white light flashed out and showed up Copan standing near the centre of the hall.

"I thought as much," came Pecos' jeering voice. "I felt sure you were not far off. Stick up your hands, you white nigger, and be quick about it. Up with them," he snarled. "There are half a dozen guns besides my own covering you.''

Copan obeyed, for there was nothing else to do. Poor Billy gasped with horror, then grabbed for his own pistol.

'' I'll get Pecos if I die for it,'' he snapped out as he sprang towards the gap.

Cottle caught him in a grip of steel and swung him aside.

'' You are crazy. They'll kill Copan first and you afterwards. This time we have to talk, not shoot.

'' You have got the better of us this time, Pecos,'' he said in a loud, clear voice. '' Still, you haven't yet got things all your own way, for Castro is our prisoner, and you don't know where to find him.''

'' Oh, don't I?'' sneered Pecos. '' He is in there with you.''

'' And if he is,'' replied Cottle calmly, '' how will that help you or him? If you try violence I can shoot him before you reach him, and if you attempt to force your way into this room I can tell you you are going to lose pretty heavily.''

'' There is no need for me to do anything of the sort,'' said Pecos with an ugly chuckle. '' If I hand over your friend here to my men I shall soon have you as well as him screaming for mercy.''

'' The swine!'' groaned Billy. '' Does he mean he'll torture Copan?''

Cottle spoke again. '' Listen to me, Pecos. I will give up Castro in exchange for Copan and for your promise that he and I and Hawkins shall be allowed to leave in the plane."

Pecos burst into harsh laughter. "You don't want much, do you?" he jeered. "Why, you fool, you are at my mercy. I have over a score of men around the place and plenty of dynamite. I'll give you your lives, and that's more than you deserve. Otherwise, unconditional surrender. Now I'm going to count ten, and if before I have finished you have not dropped your weapons and come out unarmed I shall order my men to begin work upon Copan."

For the first time since he had known him, Billy saw Cottle flinch. "My heavens!" he muttered. "I don't know what to do. It isn't as if I could trust the brute to keep his word."

Pecos began to count. "One—two—three," he recited slowly. "Four," he continued, and got no further, for suddenly the air was rent by a terrifying scream, followed by a chorus of yells which sounded like nothing human. The sounds came from outside.

"The Araks," cried Copan.

As he spoke the light of Pecos' torch fell away from him, and, spinning round, the little man came bounding back to the opening. He must have had eyes like those of a cat, for next instant he had reached the gap in the wall and was safe inside with the others.

"The Araks!" exclaimed Billy. "Those wild Indians, you mean?"

"Don't waste time talking," advised Cottle, "but help me stop this hole." From outside came a crackle of rifle shots, then more screams. Billy leaped to the window.

"My goodness! What brutes!" he gasped.

"Be careful, Billy," warned Cottle. "They can see in the dark and their arrows are poisoned." But the sight outside was so terrible yet so fascinating that Billy could not tear himself away from the window, and Cottle, too, stood beside him and watched. A fearful battle was raging in the square, where Pecos' men were making a desperate resistance.

But they had been taken by surprise, and were outnumbered twenty to one. Also, unfortunately for themselves, they were scattered. Many of the Araks went down under the drive of nickel-tipped bullets, but more and more came rushing up, while others from behind showered arrows and spears upon the wretched rebels.

Within ten minutes there was not a white man left alive, except the four in their secret hiding-place, and the savages were busy plundering the dead bodies.

"The next thing will be they'll get the plane," groaned Billy. "They can't help but see her." Almost as he spoke two of the Indians announced by shrill cries that they had found the plane, and a score or more of their companions came running up.

"That's done it," muttered Billy as he strained his eyes through the star-lit gloom. "Yes, they are all round it. Oh, I say, Professor, can't we do something."

"Nothing, I fear, Billy," replied the older man gravely.

"But the plane——" Billy was in absolute agony, for he had the true airman's love of his machine.

"They may not harm it, after all," said Cottle.

"If they don't, they'll strip it and leave it perfectly useless," declared Billy. "Look at the brutes," he went on angrily. "They are all over her."

He was right. There was starlight sufficient to see big brown men, who looked more like apes than human beings, swarming over the Dolphin. A great glare of light burst out. One of them had accidently switched on the headlight, and the others jumped back in panic.

"That's scared them," said Billy. "I say, Professor, if we open fire from the window, don't you think they would clear?"

Cottle said a few swift words to Copan, but the little man shook his head. "It would be madness," he told them, "for should they learn that we were here they would never rest until they had killed us."

"Whether they scupper us or not, this sees our finish," said Billy despondently. "Look, they are back again and pulling everything to pieces with their filthy paws. They've got hold of our grub now."

It was true. The Araks had opened the food locker and were munching cakes of chocolate. One had a tin of tongue which somehow he had ripped open. He was tearing out the contents with his fingers and thrusting them into his huge mouth. A third had got hold of the bottle of brandy carried for emergencies and was pouring it down his throat.

Billy was sick with rage. He could hardly keep from crying out. More and more of the savages were coming up. There were nearly a hundred round the plane. " There's another with a tin," said Billy. " Look at the brutes fighting for it." Half a dozen of the loathly creatures were struggling for something which they had taken out of the plane.

Between them it suddenly dropped to the ground. A fountain of fire spurted up. There was a shattering crash, and the mob of struggling Indians was ripped apart and its members flung in every direction.

" It's a bomb!" gasped Billy. " My heavens, it's a bomb, and the poor brutes thought it was a meat tin!"

The crash was followed by a deadly silence, but this lasted only a few seconds. Then, with shrieks of terror the surviving savages turned and ran for their lives. In the twinkling of an eye the street was cleared and only those who would never run again were left behind.

Billy craned forward out of the window. " She's all right," he exclaimed. " I don't believe she is damaged a bit."

He turned and ran for the opening and the others followed.

Billy was right. The bodies of the wretched Araks had received the full force of the explosion, and, barring a few small holes in her wings, the plane was unharmed. Billy sprang into the seat, switched on, pressed the self-starter, and instantly the engine began to roar in a most satisfying manner.

At the thunderous noise Copan started back.

" Is the great bird angry, my lord?" he asked of Cottle.

" No, she is only anxious to fly home!" smiled Cottle as he stowed the bag of emeralds carefully in the locker. " But how about you, old friend? Will you be safe from the Indians?"

" Thanks to you, señores, I and my people are now safe from all our enemies," said Copan gratefully. " Now I, like you, must fly home."

Without another word he melted away into the gloom and disappeared. " Good-bye, old scout," shouted Billy, but his voice was lost in the roar of the great engine.

Cottle touched him on the shoulder. " I have Castro safe," he said in the other's ear. Just to make quite sure I have tied his legs. You can start as soon as you like."

" All right," replied Billy. " I'll run her out into the square. There's just room for her to pass."

Next moment the machine began to move, and under Billy's skilful guidance shot out into the square. Her pace quickened, and as she came opposite the great statue her wheels left the ground and she lifted.

In a matter of seconds only she had risen above the roof of the great temple. Billy headed her to the south-east and away she roared through the calm night air at a speed of nearly two miles a minute.

Billy took a last glance downwards at the mysterious ruins which lay below. "I only hope old Copan gets back safely to supper," he said to Cottle. "Me, I'm thinking of breakfast to-morrow with Tenorio."

"It ought to be quite a cheerful meal," replied Cottle, and smiled as he thought of that bag of emeralds safely stowed beneath him.

THE END

They shot away down the rough track at startling speed.